ZORAN

I had to run to keep up with her. I don't kno...

got so tall. "It's humiliating," she

treats us like a bunch of kid...'

"We *are* a bunch of kids, ... because ... ly

made her crosser I added, "He's quite useful. You know,

with the Babes, and the parents away so much."

Flora shot me one of her sideways Flora looks. "I sup-

pose you like him."

I thought about Zoran making hot chocolate for us,

putting double the amount of powder in Jas's because

that's how she likes it, and about how he sat working on

his thesis in the rain when it was his turn to watch the rats.

"I don't like his beard," I said. "But I do think he's nice."

"That," said Flora, "is just typical."

OTHER BOOKS YOU MAY ENJOY

NATASHA FARRANT

PUFFIN BOOKS
imprint of Penguin Group (USA)

PUFFIN BOOKS
Published by the Penguin Group
Penguin Group (USA) LLC
375 Hudson Street
New York, New York 10014

USA ★ Canada ★ UK ★ Ireland ★ Australia
New Zealand ★ India ★ South Africa ★ China

penguin.com
A Penguin Random House Company

First published in the United States of America by Dial Books for Young Readers,
an imprint of Penguin Group (USA) Inc., 2013
Published by Puffin Books, an imprint of Penguin Young Readers Group, 2014

THE LIBRARY OF CONGRESS HAS CATALOGED THE DIAL BOOKS EDITION AS FOLLOWS:
Farrant, Natasha.
After Iris / by Natasha Farrant
p. cm.
Summary: Twelve-year-old Bluebell Gadsby's written and video diary chronicles life
in a rowdy London family, and how Zoran, the new au pair, and Joss, the troublemaking
boy next door, help to pull her out of her shell and cope with the loss of her twin
three years before.
ISBN 978-0-8037-3982-6 (hardcover)
[1. Family life—England—London—Fiction. 2. Grief—Fiction.
3. Brothers and sisters—Fiction. 4. Au pairs—Fiction.
5. Video recordings—Production and direction—Fiction.
6. Diaries—Fiction. 7. Twins—Fiction.] I. Title.
PZ7.F2406Aft 2013
[Fic]—dc23
2012039136

Puffin Books ISBN 978-0-14-242691-3

Printed in the United States of America

1 3 5 7 9 10 8 6 4 2

For my brother and sisters.

With special thanks to Justine and Lily.

AFTER IRIS

Being a combination of conventional diary entries
and transcripts of short films shot by the author on
the camera she was given for her twelfth birthday.

LONDON

THE FILM DIARIES OF BLUEBELL GADSBY
SCENE ONE (TRANSCRIPT)
ANOTHER PERFECT DAY IN PARADISE

DAYTIME. THE GADSBY FAMILY HOME. GARDEN.

CAMERAMAN (BLUEBELL) lingers on a pair of feet
in frayed canvas All Stars (her own), before panning
down stone steps to the garden where FLORA (16, her
oldest sibling) is sunbathing in a bikini. Spread around
her are her iPod, her mobile, a bottle of suntan lotion,
a bottle of water, and several magazines. She is reading a book.

Pan right, following the sound of squealing, to where
younger siblings JASMINE (8) and TWIG (10) are
playing on the swing under the plane tree. Jasmine
falls. Twig whoops. Jasmine howls. Blood pours from
her split lip, staining her torn pink dress. Twig—no
longer whooping—runs toward the house. Pan left,
back to Flora turning up the volume on her iPod, then
indoors to kitchen. Picture shakes as cameraman
(still Blue) plucks a tea towel from the cooker. Back

outdoors to close-up of Jasmine's blood-smeared face. Picture is inverted as cameraman applies the tea towel to Jasmine's lip.

JASMINE

Agh! Agh!! Agh!!!

TWIG

It's not my fault! It's not my fault!

FLORA

I AM *TRYING* TO LISTEN TO MY MUSIC!

FRIDAY, AUGUST 26 (MORNING)

Flora heard something in the kitchen this morning and said it wasn't fair to make her go down alone.

"Just because I am the oldest," Flora said, "does not mean I have to be the first to die."

So we grabbed what we could, which was a cricket bat for Twig, tennis rackets for Jas and me, and the big oar Dad got in Oxford with all his boat crew's names on it for Flora. For a family that never plays sport we have an awful lot of equipment. Jas said Dad would kill Flora if she broke the oar, and Flora said she'd remember that when her entire family had been murdered because she hadn't been properly armed. But in the end we didn't need to hit the burglar, because when we got to the kitchen he turned out to be Zoran, and even though we didn't know yet that it was him, he was wearing a flowery apron and sandals and a little goatee that made him look like Mr. Tumnus in *Narnia*, who everybody knows was on the right side in the end, even if he did have his moments.

"Who are you and what are you doing here?" demanded Flora.

"I am your new babysitter," said Zoran.

"A babysitter!" cried Flora. "But why?"

Zoran gave Jas what Dad calls *a laden look*, and she bit her lip so we couldn't see the stitches they gave her at the hospital.

"Your mother called me last night," said Zoran. "She was worried."

"But how does she even *know* you?" asked Flora.

We all stared at him. It seemed so unlikely that Mum would know someone like Zoran.

"Through your father," said Zoran.

"Ah," said Flora.

And that was that. Zoran didn't elaborate and we didn't ask.

"Let's tidy up, shall we?" he said instead. "Then we can all have breakfast."

His shoulders drooped a bit when he said the tidying up bit and looking around the kitchen, I have to say I could see why. Flora keeps her room tidy but treats the rest of the house like a squat. The rest of us just squat.

"Does *anybody* do the dishes?" Zoran gazed up at the ceiling when he said that, like God might actually care.

"They're only last night's," said Flora.

Zoran smirked as he picked up a stack of plates. I could have warned him, but I didn't. He took one step backward, landed on Twig's remote-controlled Aston Martin DB2/4 Competition Spider, and vanished in a crash of china.

Zoran announced he had concussion. The Babes (aka Twig and Jas) sat cross-legged at his feet and cut bandages out of a sheet they found in the washing machine, which Flora wound around his head while they explained about the Aston Martin.

"They're for the rats," said Jas. "We have three. White, with pink eyes."

"We use Daddy's ties to strap them in, and then we race them," said Twig. "We've got lots of different models. The Spider's mine but it's okay because you didn't damage it."

"I've got a Jag XK120," said Jas. "The rats love it, they really do."

"There!" Flora stopped winding and turned Zoran to-ward the mirror.

Zoran gasped. Jas started to cry because laughing stretched her stitches. Twig snorted so hard snot came out of his nose.

"Oh my *God!*" cried Zoran. "I look like an Egyptian mummy!"

"You said you were concussed!" protested Flora.

Zoran looked cross but Flora gave him her scrunched-up nose grin, the one that makes her look like she's about ten years old instead of sixteen. Nobody can ever resist that grin.

"Thank you for rescuing me," Zoran grumbled.

Flora started to laugh then, too, and then they were all laughing, except Zoran laughed less than the others.

"I wish I'd filmed this," I said.

They all stared at me.

"You spoke!" said Zoran. "I was wondering if you knew how."

He was standing up now and the Babes walked around and around him with a roll of toilet paper, finishing off the process Flora had started on his head. That would have made a good film, too, but what I wanted to get— what I was cross I'd missed—was that look between him and Flora, when she said she thought he was concussed and he said he looked like an Egyptian mummy.

She grinned and he melted.

That was when I knew we had nothing to fear from him.

THE FILM DIARIES OF BLUEBELL GADSBY
SCENE TWO (TRANSCRIPT)
MOTHER AND DAUGHTER

DAY. THE GADSBY GARDEN.

The garden again, this time seen from above through
the branches of the plane tree. MOTHER, barefoot
but otherwise still dressed for work, is harvesting a
lavender bush with a pair of rusty shears. When all
the stalks are cut, she crouches to gather them into a
waiting basket. She buries her face in her hands, and
her shoulders relax as she inhales the scent of the
flowers.

FLORA, also barefoot but in denim cutoffs, appears on
the stone veranda at the top of the steps. Sound does
not reach the camera, but it is obvious she is annoyed.
Mother takes a step toward her, then stops to pick a
stalk from her basket. She runs her index and thumb
along the stem to strip it of its petals, which she
crushes in her fist. She inhales again, then opens her
hand and holds it out before her. The breeze scatters

the petals. Mother squares her shoulders and turns toward her angry daughter.

Picture fades to black as CAMERAMAN (BLUE) turns camera off to climb back down to the ground.

FRIDAY, AUGUST 26 (AFTERNOON)

"He's weird," announced Flora, back in the kitchen.

"He used to be a student of your father's. He's doing his doctorate in medieval literature, and he is a very nice young man." Mum had put her shoes back on, the Louboutin pumps with the red soles, which make her look like she is taller than Flora.

They couldn't see me where I was standing just outside the door. Mum looked tiny through the camera, but I could see her hand clenching and unclenching like it often does when she is fighting with Flora.

"We don't even *need* a babysitter," shouted Flora. "I'm sixteen! In some countries I'd be married."

"He is not a babysitter, he is an au pair. And you are not in *some countries*."

Flora looked stormy and didn't say anything. Mum reached out to touch her, but she stepped away. Mum sighed.

"Now that the summer holidays are over, I am going to

be traveling again, and with your father based in Warwick of course we need a babysitter. I left your brother and sisters with you for *one day*, Flora, and Jas ended up in hospital! Zoran can help you with homework when school starts again. He's rather brilliant, your father says. And it'll be fun for Twig and Jas, like having a big brother."

"What about Blue?"

"What do you mean, what about Blue?"

"What *about* me?" I asked, and they both jumped.

"Stop creeping *up* on people!" said Flora. "And stop *looking* at everyone through that stupid camera."

"It's not on. And it's not stupid."

"You have homework, too," said Mum.

"But I never need help with it," I pointed out.

"Genius," muttered Flora, but Mum smiled at me.

"Then he will just be a presence, my darling. A happy presence."

Once upon a time, about thirteen years ago, there were two little dots that grew into grains that grew into beans then babies, and they lived in the same warm water-filled sack, where they got fed through a long tube that went straight into their stomachs. The babies grew ears and mouths and fingers and toes, and they lived curled around each other. Doctors took photographs of them and people said that they were like two peas in a pod. Even before they were born, their parents called the babies Iris and Bluebell—spring names for spring babies, they said. When it was time for them to leave the water everybody thought Bluebell would go first because she was biggest, but Iris beat her to it and shot headlong into the world so fast the midwife almost dropped her.

Grandma says that nothing could ever stop Iris rushing, not even me. It's how she was born, and nine years later it was how she died.

Iris has been dead for three years. Flora cried and cried when it happened, but I'm not sure she ever thinks about her now. Not the way I do. Sometimes I dream that we're still sleeping curled around each other, and when I wake up my arms are reaching out for her. Once when Grandma was staying with us after the funeral, she said that sometimes people don't have to speak to each other to know what they are thinking, and that Iris and I had a special bond because we were twins. She said that when soldiers had limbs amputated in the war, they could still feel the arm or leg or foot that had been cut off and that this was what losing Iris was like for me. She said the memory of Iris would always be with me.

"Like a soldier without a foot," Flora said. "Blue will have to hop," she added, but Grandma said that wasn't what she meant at all.

At first when Iris died I used to see her everywhere. She felt so close I used to think our shadows had gotten mixed up. Sometimes now, if the sun is behind me when I am filming and I can see my own shadow I still pretend it's hers, but it's not the same, and Mum going on about big brothers and happy presences makes me want to scream, because I know that's not what she's really talking about, what she's really talking about is Iris and her unhappy absence.

THE FILM DIARIES OF BLUEBELL GADSBY
SCENE THREE (TRANSCRIPT)
THE BANK HOLIDAY FAMILY PICNIC

DAY. SOME RANDOM PICNIC SPOT IN THE COUNTRY.

A tablecloth is spread beneath an oak tree. Bread,
cheese, deli tubs of hummus, olives, and vine leaves.
Tomatoes, ham, squashed strawberries in a Tupper-
ware container. A half-empty bottle of white wine.
FATHER lies on his back with a battered straw hat
over his face. He wears crumpled chinos, a cotton shirt
without a collar, and a tweed jacket with leather elbow
patches. MOTHER lies beside him, leaning back on her
elbows, watching JASMINE and TWIG build a den on
the edge of the nearby woods. FLORA sits cross-legged
with her back to them, listening to her iPod. White
noise crackles around her. Father awakens, removes
the hat from his face, and sits up. He is unshaven and
has bags under his eyes.

> FATHER
> Dear child, must you make that ghastly noise?

Flora ignores him, nodding her head to the music. Father tiptoes over and removes earbuds from her ears.

FATHER
There is a reason they are called personal stereos.

FLORA
(screeches and tries to grab back earbuds)
Nobody calls them personal stereos!

CAMERAMAN (BLUE) snorts. All eyes turn to her. Mother looks worried. Father rubs his face, raises his eyebrows, and tries to stifle a yawn.

FLORA
(angrily)
Turn that camera *off*!

BLUE
(bravely)
It's for my video diary.

FLORA
Turn it off *now* or I'll throw it in the pond.

My plan is to record my life through words and images. I am using video footage for the images and some spoken words. There are not many spoken words in the video footage, because usually when people realize I am filming, they stop talking. Dad says that by the time I am grown up people will be so used to seeing me with a camera in my hand they won't be able to *stop* talking, and that I will make my fortune as a TV interviewer. But Dad says a lot of things. In the meantime, what I can't record on film, I write about on what he calls "a contemporary echo of the old-fashioned notebook"—my laptop, recently inherited from Flora.

When I write, nobody can tell me to get lost. So I have lots of mini-films, for atmosphere, plus their transcripts on the laptop, as well as longer chapters for detail. It is a multimedia record. I have seen installations like this in the Tate Modern, where Dad takes me sometimes when he says home is just too much.

Just when things were getting interesting this afternoon, what with Flora screeching and Dad looking lost, Mum made me turn the camera off. I tried to explain—again—about the plan to record my life, and that I write about everything I don't film anyway, but Flora said she didn't care.

"I don't have to read your stupid diary," she said. "But you're not filming me without any makeup."

"Try to be nice," said Mum. "A few more days and you'll be back at school."

"Thank GOD!" cried Flora.

Dad beamed and said, "Do I detect the late blooming of an academic?" and this time it was Flora who snorted.

"I think Flora is mainly looking forward to seeing her friends," murmured Mum.

"Can you blame me?" cried Flora. She pulled her mobile out of her pocket and groaned. "All my friends get home today and I'm stuck up a hill with no network and nobody to talk to."

"You could talk to us," suggested Mum. "Or go for a walk with Blue."

"Blue!" said Flora, and after that nobody talked. Which was a shame, because tomorrow Mum is flying to Moscow and Dad is driving a hundred miles back to Warwick, with us children left in the frankly dubious care of Zoran until school starts on Thursday.

When we were little, Flora used to read Iris and me stories. She even had baths with us. Our nursery was next to her primary school, and we used to wait for her at the gate with Mum. On the day we started primary at Saint Swithins, it was Flora not Mum who took us to our classroom, holding our hands all the way, not caring if she didn't look cool in front of her friends (except Flora always looks cool). It was Flora who punched Digby Jones when he laughed at me because of my glasses, and Flora who complained to the headmaster when Mrs. Fraser, my teacher in Year 2, said my reading wasn't good enough. She told him I could read by the time I went into kindergarten, and that the reason I didn't concentrate in Literacy was because at home I was already reading Charles Dickens. Which wasn't exactly true, but it was nice of her to say so.

Now all I get is: "Blue!"

TUESDAY, AUGUST 30 (MORNING)

Breakfast was interrupted this morning by Twig, shouting. He was at the bottom of the garden jumping up and down by the rat run, but when we got there he couldn't talk, only point.

"*What?*" yelled Flora.

"Are they dead?" cried Jas.

"They've *multiplied*!" screamed Twig.

We all stared, and he was right. Last night there were only three rats but this morning there were seven, including four very tiny ones. No one said anything for a while.

"But they were all girls," whispered Jas at last.

"Well they can't have been," said Zoran.

"Perhaps they're lesbians," suggested Flora.

"How would *that* work?" I asked.

We stared some more. The rats were all nestled together in a heap in the straw, and the sun made crisscross shadows over them through the wire of their cage.

"So which one's the boy?" asked Twig.

"Male," said Zoran. "Not boy."

"And which one's the mother?" Flora crouched to peer more closely. "You must have noticed she was getting fat."

But all the adult rats looked enormous.

"If you watch them long enough," said Zoran, "the mother will start nursing."

"Are they ill?" asked Twig.

"He means she'll start feeding them" said Flora. "From her breasts."

"Rats have *breasts*?" Jas looked horrified.

"Not as such," sighed Zoran.

"Can you look?" asked Twig. "Can you look underneath and see which one is the mother?"

And I bet Mum never told Zoran about this when he came for the job, that one day he might have to hold a rat upside down to work out if it had just given birth. He sighed again and looked depressed.

"I'm not sure I know how," he said.

"Will you film them, Blue?" asked Jas. "Please?"

I don't film animals. It's a matter of principle. They're

pretty and everything, but they are not as interesting to me as people, and I don't like that they can't speak. If Flora doesn't like me filming, she tells me to get lost, or she hits me. All a rat can do is hide in its bedding and even then I can always film the straw.

Jas was doing that cat thing, when her eyes go all around with the pupils very black. Her dress was torn at the shoulder and held together with a safety pin. Jas has a wardrobe full of dresses, but this has been her favorite for years and she won't wear anything else. It's pink, very faded, and only reaches about halfway down her thighs. Also, since last week, it has bloodstains down the front. She has a scab on her right knee, and she hasn't brushed her hair since the beginning of the summer. Mum tried to make her at first, but Jas dug her heels in and when Jas does that it's best to just say yes.

Jas's big cat eyes mean more or less the same as her dug-in heels. And it *was* sweet, the way she and Twig were looking at the baby rats. They sat cross-legged by the pen, whispering to them.

"Wake up, wake up," they said. "Open your eyes."

I don't think rats can even *hear* when they're this small, let alone understand English, but try telling an eight- and ten-year-old that. I didn't want to film the rats, but I did want to catch the Babes looking at them. I left them where they were—Jas and Twig on the ground, Flora on the swing,

Zoran looking glum—and I picked my way over the damp grass to fetch my camera in the house. A shadow flitted across the lawn—I just caught it out of the corner of my eye. I know it sounds mad but I swear it was human.

"Iris?" I whispered, but it didn't make sense, and by the time I got to where the shadow had been, it had gone.

THE FILM DIARIES OF BLUEBELL GADSBY
SCENE FOUR (TRANSCRIPT)
THE SEXUAL IDENTIFICATION OF RATS

INSIDE THE GADSBY HOUSE/THE GADSBY GARDEN

The picture jerks up and down as CAMERAMAN
(BLUE) runs, randomly settling on: bare feet, a flash
of wall, stairs, the black-and-white marble of the hall,
the stone veranda, gravel, a tree, grass.

> TWIG
> Blue, hurry, *hurry!*

> BLUE
> I'm *coming!!*

Picture steadies as cameraman stops running and
settles—again—on the rats' pen.

> TWIG AND JAS
> (in unison, jumping up and down)
> LOOK! LOOK! LOOK!

The picture loses focus as cameraman crouches to look. JAWS, THE GREAT WHITE RAT, (so named for once trying to take off Twig's finger) stares back. Around its neck is a tag made of wood, tied on with garden twine. The camera zooms in. The writing on the tag comes into focus.

IT SAYS:
I AM THE DADDY

WEDNESDAY, AUGUST 31

"But what a peculiar thing to write!" said Zoran.

It was very early in the morning—again—and still damp outside. After inspecting the pen, we went back to the kitchen, where Zoran made hot chocolate and Flora groaned under the duvet she had dragged downstairs with her.

"Is that all you can say?" she said. *"What a peculiar thing to write?"*

"Well it is," said Zoran.

"The weird thing," cried Flora, "the creepy, freaky thing is that somebody is obviously watching us and has broken into the rat run!"

I don't know if anyone else saw Zoran's mouth twitch.

"Was it you?" I asked.

"Me?" he said. "Go near that monster?"

"Then *who*?" demanded Jas, and Twig repeated *who who who*?

The weather has changed and it rained all day, but we all took turns watching the rat run, even Flora, who huddled under the umbrella in a blanket with more hot chocolate and a book and said she'd like to catch the so-and-so who was spying on us and give him a piece of her mind. Those were her actual words. She sounded like Grandma.

And obviously we never saw the spy.

Tomorrow we go back to school. I have never looked forward to anything less in my entire life. Dad always says that anything is possible. Perhaps this term things will be different, but somehow I doubt it.

THURSDAY, SEPTEMBER 1

Since Iris died, at school *I* am the shadow. I slip down corridors, from assembly to class to break and back to class, and no one sees me, no one talks to me. People who have known me since primary school, people I've peed with in paddling pools and who have smeared my face in birthday cake—they squeal when they see each other and fall into one another's arms, they giggle and whisper, but with me they just go blank and I know that nothing has changed.

Just for a moment this morning, I thought things might be different. I caught Dodi Cartwright's eye in assembly and I was pretty sure she acknowledged me—not much, a sort of half dip of the head, an almost smile. But then in our first class, which was English, I was going to sit down near the window at the back, when Dodi shimmied in and parked herself on my chair. I did try to say something. I thought, *what would Flora do now*, and I tried to say *hey, Cartwright, get lost that was my seat*, but no words came out, and even if they had there wouldn't have been any point because by then everyone was crowded around listening to her yammer on about her summer holiday in Italy or Spain or somewhere. So I just picked up my stuff and slunk off to the only free desk, which was right at the front next to Jake Lyall, who has to sit there because the teachers say they have to keep an eye on him, and was actually asleep so couldn't have spoken to me even if he'd wanted to, which he probably didn't.

We have Miss Foundry in English, who is insane even by Clarendon Free School standards. Today she wore a beaded shawl which reached down to her ankles, told us to call her Anthea, and tried to recruit us for the Clarendon Players' Christmas Extravaganza.

"This term," she announced, "they will be doing tales from the Brothers Grimm!"

Everybody looked blank.

"The brothers who?" yawned Jake.

"Snow White! Hansel and Gretel! Little Red Riding Hood!" cried Miss Foundry.

"What's she on about?" asked Tom Myers.

"Jacob and Wilhelm Grimm," said Hattie Verney, confirming that she is going to be just as much of a know-it-all in Year 9 as she was in Year 8. "Together they collected and rewrote over two hundred traditional folktales, some of which we know today through Disney adaptations."

Tom pulled a face at her. Miss Foundry pretended not to notice.

"As usual, the Clarendon Players are looking to local schools to swell the ranks of their Christmas production. Bluebell, dear, will Flora be taking part?"

Cressida Taylor, who is Dodi's best friend, snickered *Bluebell* like it was the most idiotic name on the planet. Which, of course, it is.

"I suppose so, miss," I stammered. Flora has been taking part in the Players' productions pretty much since she could walk. Her dream is to be discovered, leave school, appear in a West End show, and then be whisked off to Broadway.

"Please, dear, call me Anthea."

"Antheaaaaahhh," said Tom, and Miss Foundry ignored him again.

"What about you, dear?" she asked. "Will you audition?"

"What, *her*?" sneered Cressida.

"No, miss," I said.

Anthea looked worried and sad and disappointed. All at once.

Dad says there are victims in life and there are fighters. He says he hopes that we will always be fighters, and by lunchtime I'd had enough. There was no way I was going to give Cressida and Dodi the satisfaction of seeing me eat alone. It wasn't difficult to slip out with a group of older kids. Most of them didn't notice me but those who did sort of fell in around me so the teacher on gate duty didn't see. Which considering it was Madame Gilbert didn't really matter anyway.

I ate tomato soup and bread and butter in a café off Portobello Road. The café is called Home Sweet Home, and it was full of mothers with strollers and workmen in overalls and people with black-rimmed glasses reading iPads. A very old Labrador panted by the counter. Capital was on the radio, and the whole place smelled of chips and coffee and wet dog. Nobody spoke to me, but it didn't matter because nobody was meant to.

Madame Gilbert was talking loudly into her mobile in French when I got back. I wasn't supposed to be out but then she wasn't supposed to be on the phone, so she just looked vague and waved me in. We reviewed fractions in maths. Dull, but so, so easy. I slept all the way through, and Mr. Forsyth (aka Mr. Math) didn't even notice.

Like I said. Totally invisible.

THURSDAY, SEPTEMBER 1/FRIDAY, SEPTEMBER 2 (THE MIDDLE OF THE NIGHT)

I am sitting on the flat roof outside my bedroom window, and I am very cold.

At dinner (sausages and mash—Zoran doesn't cook anything else and he gets really hurt if you complain) Twig said we should be watching the rats *twenty-four/seven*. His words. He said it was only luck that nothing else had happened since last time. Jas said what about when we are at school, and Twig said Zoran could watch them then. Zoran said he had to go to classes too, and he couldn't just sit around here all day waiting for us to come back, and he had a thesis to write or didn't we know? Jas said no, she didn't know and what's a thesis, and then Twig said, what about when we are asleep?

"Last time he came at night," said Twig.

"He's only been once," said Flora. "And he might be a she."

"Even so. It doesn't mean he won't come again, and when he does, I bet it'll be when we're in bed."

"You can't stay up all night," said Zoran. "I expressly forbid it."

Zoran has been trying to assert his authority all evening because Mum e-mailed this morning to say she wasn't coming home between Moscow and New York, and Flora went to her friend Tamsin's after school where she dyed her hair bright pink and also dreadlocked it using a kit Tam's brother had ordered on the Internet.

Really. Pink dreadlocks. Zoran went ballistic.

"And another thing." Twig pushed his plate aside, brought it back for a last mouthful of sausage, and hopped off his chair. "We haven't even looked for clues."

"Oh God," Flora groaned.

"Blue?" Twig doesn't do the round cat eye thing like Jas, but his lower lip wobbles when he wants something and you just can't say no.

"Oh, go on then," I sighed.

We all went, even Zoran, who after only a week has pretty much given up on the washing up. Flora insists there's no point doing the dishes at night because what if you die when you're asleep, so now he makes us take turns doing them in the morning. We crossed the lawn and stood by the pen and Twig gave us our orders, which were basically *leave no stone unturned*.

"That child watches too much television," grumbled Flora.

It was Jas who found the footprints. There was nothing on the lawn or the gravel—nothing we could see, anyway, and it *had* been raining—but right in the far corner, behind the rhododendrons, at the bottom of the Batemans' wall, there were two deep marks of somebody's trainers.

"Male, I should think." Zoran was getting into the swing of the whole detective thing. "Judging from the size. And they're facing the wall, which suggests he jumped down or climbed up here."

"Mr. *Bateman*?" cried Jas.

"He's, like, a hundred and three," Flora explained to Zoran.

"He would *die* if he jumped this fence," said Twig.

"So there must be somebody else."

Zoran wanted to go around to the Batemans to talk about it but we said no, we'd known them all our lives and it would be too embarrassing. He sighed (in actually a very *non*authoritarian way) and asked what we wanted to do, and we sort of shuffled around and said nothing, it didn't matter.

So here I am. Sitting on the flat roof. Freezing my little socks off in the middle of the night.

I took over from Flora at one o'clock. We're doing two-hour shifts.

I love London at night. At Grandma's, in Devon, the night is as black as coal and the stars are brighter, but it's creepily quiet. Here you can still hear the traffic, and the sky is dark but orange, and even though most people are asleep you can still feel the life of the place because it never completely stops. Grandma calls London *THAT STINK-HOLE* and says she can't understand how we can survive here for even a minute. She says that leaving London after Gramps retired was the best thing she did in her entire life, but every morning last spring we saw a fox sunbathing on the roof of the Batemans' shed. In the summer, you can lie on your back on the lawn and watch the swifts, and on weekends you can smell barbecues going all the way down the street.

I just saw something move.

THE FILM DIARIES OF BLUEBELL GADSBY
SCENE FIVE (TRANSCRIPT)
THE SPY IN OUR MIDST

NIGHT. THE GADSBY GARDEN, SEEN FROM THE
FLAT ROOF OUTSIDE BLUE'S ROOM.

The lawn is black and still, the lavender, lilac and
ceanothus which border it are dark twisted masses.
The plane tree at the bottom of the garden sways in
the wind and the rhododendrons tremble. Beyond the
garden, more darkness stretches to the row of terraced
houses in the next street, identical to this one—four
stories high, brown brick at the back and white stucco
at the front. An occasional square of light where curtains are not drawn, occupants not sleeping. Walls of
the same brown brick surround the garden, topped
with solid square trellis. A crouched figure is running
along the right-hand wall.

He wears dark clothes and a beanie on his head. The
camera follows him to the end of the wall, where he
hurdles overlapping branches. He slips off the wall into

the rhododendrons and darkness. There is no sound
but CAMERAMAN breathing, no image but the garden.

The rhododendrons shake, and the figure is back, bent
double as he (definitely a he) runs back toward the
camera. There is a gap in the trellis a few feet from
the house, just wide enough to get a hold on the wall,
or to launch off it. The figure stops, turns, prepares to
jump, then stops again. He turns back toward the garden and looks straight up at the camera. Removes his
beanie and gives a little bow. Stands up straight again.
Replaces the beanie.

Waves.

Then jumps, and disappears.

FRIDAY, SEPTEMBER 2

"But why didn't you come and *get* us?" wailed Jas. "We
could have caught him!"

"Don't be absurd," said Flora. "You can see for yourself,
he'd already gone."

"I did come and find you," I said. "You were asleep."

They all piled into my bed at dawn this morning, the

Babes dragging Flora, demanding to know what happened to their watch.

"Not necessary," I told them. "I got him."

"Show us," ordered Twig.

And there was that face again—I'd looked at it several times already before going to sleep. Messy hair, wicked grin, with a look of owning the world.

"He looks nice," said Jas.

"He looks weird," said Twig.

"He's quite good looking," admitted Flora.

"Blue?" asked Jas.

"He looks interesting," I said.

"What was he *doing* this time, anyway?" said Flora.

"The rats!" Twig froze. Literally. His face went white and his body went stiff, then he threw himself off the bed and pounded down the stairs.

"Oh, God," sighed Flora. "More rodent drama."

"I thought you *cared*," said Jas.

"I don't like being spied on," said Flora. "I couldn't care less about the rats."

This time there were ribbons tied around the rats who aren't the daddy—two pink ones for Betsy and Petal, the two fat adults who aren't Jaws, three blue and one pink for the babies. Which is no small feat, considering how tiny they are.

"It is a mystery," said Zoran, "who would do such a thing."

"We know!" chirped Twig, and then Zoran made us tell him everything and yelled at us for staying up and not following orders.

"Ignore him," said Flora. "He can't hit us; he's not our father."

"He couldn't hit us even if he *was* our father," said Jas. "It's actually illegal."

"I am *trying* to *protect* you." Zoran sank into the kitchen sofa and put his head in his hands.

"Pathetic," muttered Flora, but Jas threw her arms around Zoran's neck to say sorry, and then Twig said he was sorry, too, and after a minute so did I.

"*Completely* pathetic," grumbled Flora. She picked up her schoolbag. "Come on, Blue."

I had to run to keep up with her. I don't know when she got so tall. "It's humiliating," she raged as we walked. "He treats us like a bunch of kids."

"We *are* a bunch of kids," I said, then because that only made her crosser I added, "He's quite useful. You know, with the Babes, and the parents away so much."

Flora shot me one of her sideways Flora looks. "I suppose you like him."

I thought about Zoran making hot chocolate for us, putting double the amount of powder in Jas's because that's how she likes it, and about how he sat working on his thesis in the rain when it was his turn to watch the rats.

"I don't like his beard," I said. "But I do think he's nice."

"That," said Flora, "is just typical."

"I hate school," I said.

"What's that got to do with anything?"

I wanted to ask her if she remembered lying to the headmaster at Saint Swithin's about me reading Dickens when I was five, but I could tell she wasn't in the mood. She flitted off to join her friends as soon as we reached the gates, and I knew she probably wouldn't notice if I spent the rest of the day screaming naked in the playground.

No chance of skipping out at lunchtime with Mr. Math on the door. Flora nabbed me as I slunk into the canteen.

"He's here!" she hissed.

"People are staring," I said, and to be honest I'm not surprised. Flora is widely regarded as one of the coolest girls in school, but the pink dreads do take getting used to.

"If it's all the same to you," I said, "*I* am doing my best not to stand out."

"He's here!" she repeated. "He's in my year!"

"*Who* is here?"

"Who d'you think? The spy! The rat boy!"

"Are you sure?"

"He *introduced* himself! 'I believe we're neighbors,' he said, then he took his hat off like he did in the video."

"What's he like?"

"Quite cute, to be fair, but God he fancies himself. *I believe we're neighbors*—who even talks like that? He actually *winked* at me!"

"We *are* neighbors," I pointed out, but Flora wasn't listening.

"Whoa," she said. "They really are looking at us."

I swear the whole canteen was in shock, like they'd just worked out we were related. Candy-Floss Head and Little Miss Nobody.

"Gotta run," said Flora.

"Can I have lunch with you?"

"Sorry, tadpole," she said. "I'm going out."

I wanted to bail then, spend lunch in the toilets or the library or something, but I was too hungry. I needn't have worried anyway. With Flora gone, people lost interest. I carried my tray to an empty table and tried to look like I was eating alone by choice.

I stood up to clear my tray when I finished and froze.

The boy from next door sat alone on the other side of the room, and he was staring straight at me.

It's warmer tonight. Zoran has said that even though he is not our father he will personally whip us if we keep watch again, but I couldn't sleep so I climbed out of my window onto the flat roof like I did last night. I sat with my duvet around my shoulders, and in the moonlight my shadow looked like a giant mushroom with my head a little bobble on top. I slid my hand out from under the duvet and moved it like the Indian dancers Dad took me to see last winter, then pinched my fingers and thumb together to look like a duck.

I waved, and the mushroom waved back. I shook my head and the mushroom's hair went wild. I held out my hand, and the shadow of another hand reached out and touched mine.

I have never moved so fast in my entire life. I dived through the open window—literally, headfirst. I'd have made it, too, if I hadn't tried to take the duvet with me. As it was, Joss Bateman caught hold of it (the duvet) and pulled, and we ended up sitting on either side of the window, me inside, him out.

"Sorry I scared you," he said.

Flora always says you should never admit to being frightened. Or weak. Or to feeling stupid. She says if people know any of these things about you, they will take advantage. So even though I must have looked completely petrified, sitting there on the floor of my bedroom hugging my duvet and eyeing the open window like it was some portal I had to close against the Forces of Darkness, I still said, "I'm not scared."

"I just wanted to meet you."

What I should have said is, that it was a bit weird climbing onto people's roofs like a burglar in the middle of the night just because you're after an introduction, but I didn't think of that until later. As in right now.

"Oh." Is what I actually said.

"Did you like what I did with the rats?" he asked.

"Um," I said.

"The sight of you all." He grinned. "Sitting there in the rain waiting for me to come back! I nearly died it was so funny."

"Hilarious," I croaked.

"I don't mean to be rude," he said.

"Well you are," I said. And then I yanked the duvet in and slammed the window shut. He pressed his face against the glass, but I closed the curtains. Then I ran to my bed and pulled the covers over my head until I heard him leave.

SATURDAY, SEPTEMBER 3

Flora is ecstatic because Greg, the director of the Clarendon Players, told her that this year she could audition for a speaking part. The auditions were this morning, and she came back glowing because she is going to play Snow White. Twig said, "Snow White? But she's such a drip!" and

Jas said, "Don't they mind about your hair?" Flora said it was completely typical of her family to be so unsupportive and that her Snow White was going to be unlike any other the world had ever seen.

"Greg says I am the perfect person to inject personality into the role," she announced, and then she went on and on about how she is the youngest member of the speaking cast and how there were going to be film scouts and agents and everything on the opening night and how this was the beginning of the sparkling career in show business which was going to take her away from her humdrum schoolgirl existence.

Or something like that.

"So I spoke to Mr. Bateman," said Zoran when she stopped for breath. "The boy is their grandson. He is going to Clarendon Free School."

"We knew *that* already," said Flora.

"Doesn't he mind?" asked Jas. "Being sent away from his parents?"

"From what I gathered," said Zoran, "things are not easy for him at home."

"Why not?" asked Twig, but apparently Mr. Bateman didn't say and Zoran didn't like to ask.

"Should I tell him about last night?" I asked Flora when Zoran had gone upstairs.

"What, that our psycho neighbor's crawling all over

the roof trying his hand at breaking and entering?"

I shrugged.

"He'll only make a fuss," Flora sighed, "and then we'd have Mum and Dad on our backs."

"Maybe they'd come home," I said, and she gave me another Flora look.

"They'd only leave again," she said.

This is what happened with Mum and Dad.

Seventeen years ago, when Cassie (Mum) had just started work at L'Oréal in London and David (Dad) was finishing his doctorate in medieval literature at Oxford, they went to Glastonbury. And even though they had been to Glastonbury every summer for years and had never met, this time they pitched their tents side by side. It rained. Cassie's tent collapsed. David and his mates invited Cassie and her friends into theirs. He played his guitar in the tent and sang "Moon River." She told him that ever since she saw Audrey Hepburn sing it in *Breakfast at Tiffany's*, which was her favorite movie, it was her favorite song.

After that they went to the cinema every night for two weeks, and with every new film they fell a little bit more in love. David loved the movies even more than medieval literature, and Cassie definitely loved them more than L'Oréal. Two weeks later, in the middle of a Quentin Tarantino double bill, between *Reservoir Dogs* and *Pulp Fiction* (both films they have forbidden us to watch), David proposed.

Luckily, because David and Cassie were quite poor, David's father had pots of money from working in the city before he and Grandma retired to go and live in Devon. So David and Cassie brushed the popcorn off their clothes and went to see him and Grandma, and told them that not only were they gaining a daughter but they were also going to be grandparents, and Grandpa bought them the house on Chatsworth Square where we still live now, which is old and drafty though apparently quite valuable.

Grandma also dusted down Dad's old nanny, who came to look after Flora while Cassie carried on climbing the ladder of the cosmetics industry, and Dad, who had always secretly dreamed of becoming a famous film director, became a teacher at Goldsmiths and wrote books that nobody ever read except his students because he made them. And then Dad's nanny retired for the second time, and Iris and I were born, and Mum stopped work, and three years later Twig came along, and then Jas, and even though Iris died everything was *fine* until last year when Dad announced he had this job in Warwick which was a promotion and they had a row which we weren't meant to hear but did. The row was all about Mum going mad stuck at home all day thinking about Iris and Dad saying let's move to Warwick, we all need a fresh start, and Mum saying over her dead body and she had a right to a life, too, and then she cried and the next thing we knew she told us she had a job and was flying to New York for training with Bütylicious.

Bütylicious is based in New York but has offices all over the world that she has to visit all the time, for reasons she has tried to explain but none of us understand. So then there was Katya, who was Lithuanian and couldn't cook; and Eva, who was Slovakian and homesick; and that took us up to the beginning of this summer, when we went to Devon to stay with Grandma. And now we have Zoran, and Dad's in Warwick even on the weekends, and Mum Skypes us from China as long as it's not too late and this is just how things are and there is absolutely no point in Flora getting cross about it or dyeing her hair pink.

THURSDAY, SEPTEMBER 15

Rain. Rain. Rain.

Today none of the older kids went out at lunchtime. Flora and all her noisy friends took over half the canteen and the rest of us had to squeeze up like sardines in a tin, except I found a table on my own in the corner where I can watch people but they can't see me because I'm hiding behind a pillar, and that is when I saw Joss Bateman again. He was in the lunch line, also alone, but somehow his aloneness was different than mine because he didn't look invisible, he just looked like he couldn't care less. Graham Lewis, who Flora says is an idiot and nobody likes, tried to sneak past him in the queue. Joss stuck his foot out and everyone laughed their heads off at the sight of Graham lying on the floor covered in chips, but Joss just sort of smiled and stepped over him like he wasn't even there, and the next thing I knew I heard the scrape of a chair being pulled back and his voice above me saying *do you mind if I sit here* and I looked up and there he was.

"Yes," I said.

"Tough," he said, and sat down anyway.

We didn't talk. He was eating the pasta bake, and I just focused on my rice pudding. However much I hate Clarendon Free School, you have to hand it to them, they make a mean rice pudding. I tried to ignore Joss but then he coughed, and when I looked up he had stuck his spoon on his nose. He looked completely ridiculous.

"That's better," he said. "You're even prettier when you smile."

Which was really cheesy (as well as a lie—I am never pretty). I would have left except he sat back in his chair with his arms crossed and these long, long legs stretched out in front of him, looking like he just *expected* conversation.

"Popularity," said Joss Bateman, "is a mystery."

"Yes," I agreed, because I have often thought this.

"But usually, if a person is *un*popular, it's for a reason."

I said nothing.

"Take you, for example," he argued. "You're a nice kid, you don't smell or dress like a freak. And yet here you are. Alone."

"Not *completely* alone," I mumbled.

"Alone until I got here," said Joss. "You also go to class alone and spend recess in the library. Don't argue. You know I've been watching you."

"That doesn't mean . . ."

"There's got to be a reason for it," said Joss.

Behind him, at the Year 10 table, Flora was waving her hands above her head. "Are you okay?" she mouthed. Joss turned, just in time to see Flora clutch her throat and pretend to choke.

"Is she always like that?" he asked. If he guessed that Flora's gagging had anything to do with him, he didn't seem to mind. He actually looked like he thought it was funny.

"Always," I said. I couldn't help smiling, even though a moment before I wanted to cry, because that is the thing with Flora. However annoying she is, she can always make you smile when you need her to.

"What do you want?" I asked Joss.

"To rescue you," he said. He leaned back in his chair so

it was tipping back on two legs, and grinned. "I'm your knight in shining armor."

What with Dad being a professor of medieval literature, our family knows a lot about knights in shining armor. All our games when we were little were about Merlin and Arthur and Lancelot and the evil Morgan Le Fay.

Even in our wildest imagination they never wore hoodies and high-tops.

THE FILM DIARIES OF BLUEBELL GADSBY
SCENE SIX (TRANSCRIPT)
LOSING TWIG

DAYTIME. A PACKED TRAIN ON THE LONDON
UNDERGROUND.

ZORAN hangs onto an overhead handrail, reading a
folded newspaper. Around him, a gaggle of tourists
shove and screech and laugh. A toddler screams to be
allowed out of his stroller. His mum jangles keys in
front of his face then ignores him when he screams
louder. A girl with a silver nose ring snogs a boy with
a dragon tattoo. Camera lingers on them and the girl
gives it the finger. Camera returns to Zoran, dips to
reveal JASMINE, clinging to his jacket then pans left
to TWIG, who moves his lips as he reads a poem on
the ad space above his head. The train pulls into South
Kensington station and the picture blurs as passengers
fight their way off. Zoran and Jas erupt onto the platform on a wave of gesticulating Italians.

ZORAN

(folds his newspaper)

All present and correct?

JASMINE

(clutches Zoran's arm as train doors close)

Twig's still on the train!

ZORAN

(very pale)

Christ! God! Jesus! No!

JASMINE

Twig! Twig! Oh, Twig!

ZORAN

It's okay, he'll just get on the next train back.
We'll wait for him on the platform.

CAMERAMAN (BLUE)

Did you tell him to do that?

ZORAN

What?

CAMERAMAN (BLUE)

Just, he'd never think of doing it on his own.

JASMINE

(rolls on the ground, tears streaming down her cheeks)

We've lost Twig forever!

UNIFORMED OFFICIAL

What's going on 'ere then?

ZORAN

We have lost a child!

UNIFORMED OFFICIAL

Turn the camera off, miss.

SATURDAY, SEPTEMBER 17

Twig was fine. Obviously. He pulled the emergency cord as soon as he realized we had got off the train without him, and then when all hell broke loose at the next stop and the transport police tried to work out what the emergency was, the nose bar and tattoo couple bundled him onto a train going the other way and brought him back to South

Ken. The whole thing took precisely seven minutes.

Twig was all *I don't know why you were so worried*, and Jas sobbed even louder and said he was stupid and she hated him and then the uniformed official said *there there, little girl*, and Jas looked like she might bite him. And Zoran said he was sorry but he had to go to the pub where we all had Cokes except for Zoran who ordered a double vodka, which he drank in one go. And then we went to the Natural History Museum, because that's why we were in South Ken in the first place, to visit the Darwin wing for Twig's science project, where I had the weirdest conversation with Zoran over a blue morpho butterfly, which started with me saying I hate the way they pin butterflies onto boards.

"The pins are not the worst part," said Zoran.

"They are for me," I said.

I held out my hand and traced the contours of the morpho through the glass of its case. When I looked up Zoran was still standing there, watching me.

"Little Blue," he said. Just that. *Little Blue.*

"I was thinking," Zoran continued, "how strange that the butterfly carries your name."

"Hardly," I said. "And I am not little," I added.

"You are little to me. And you're right, it's not strange. Maybe it's appropriate. I hope that one day you too will learn to fly."

Like I said. Weird.

Mum came back from China this morning very early. She took us all out for breakfast, and then she went to football with Twig and watched a DVD with Jas and ate the lunch that Zoran cooked (sausage soup—what a surprise). Then she started to sway and said she thought she had better go to bed and that was when Zoran said he would take us all to the museum, except Flora who had a rehearsal and wouldn't have come anyway. I went in to see her—Mum, I mean—when we got back, and she was sitting on the side of the bed, trying to get up and looking like she had been crying.

Later Flora said guess what, Dad called to say he couldn't come home this weekend because he has to do extra work on his latest unreadable book, and Mum took it really badly. And even though Flora and I don't agree about much these days, we both thought she was being a bit dramatic. If we cried every time our parents didn't come home when they said they would, we would drown in a vale of tears, as Grandma would say. And we always knew Dad wouldn't be home this weekend—he was all vague on the phone when Jas asked him. Flora said he probably has a girlfriend and that this is the Beginning of the End, then got cross because Jas believed her. Jas asked, what did I think, and I said I didn't know and then Flora said, "For God's sake, Blue, for once in your life get off the fence."

Mum is still on Asia time and got up at the crack of dawn, which meant that Jas and Twig did, too, because they both insisted on sleeping with her last night.

Zoran had the day off today and left early without saying where he was going. At lunch we talked about Joss and the rats, Twig on the Tube, and Flora's hair. All things, says Flora, we couldn't really talk about in front of Zoran, because he really should have told the parents about them himself except we begged him not to but now that Mum's here we want her to know anyway.

"I know you probably hate it now, but look."

Flora undid the scarf that holds her dreadlocks up and they fell down her back like a curtain of puce. "Isn't it *dramatic?*"

"It's certainly a statement," said Mum.

"The babies are so cute," said Jas. "Don't you think they're cute, Mummy?"

"Adorable," said Mum.

"I wasn't frightened at all," said Twig. "It was nice to be on my own for once."

"You and the thousand other people on the Tube," said Flora.

"What kind people to bring you back," said Mum.

"I'm thinking of adding red streaks," said Flora.

"Zoran says we have to separate them," said Jas. "He says otherwise we will be overrun by rat babies and that would be unhygienic."

"I *was* alone," grumbled Twig, "because I didn't *know* anybody."

"Or purple would be good," said Flora.

"But they *love* each other," cried Jas. "It's cruel to separate people who love each other."

"They're rats," snapped Flora. "Not people."

"I think Zoran's right, darling," said Mum. "You can have too many rats."

"But what about Daddy!" Jas burst into tears. "He's not here, and it's *miserable!*"

And then there was lots of cuddling Jas, and Flora stomping about because no one cared about the red or pink, and Twig sulking because no one understood him. By the time she got to me she was so frazzled—her word—she just collapsed on my bed and we didn't have a good conversation at all.

"Thank goodness for my sensible Blue," she said between two yawns, and I didn't answer because who, in the history of families, wanted to be *the sensible one*?

"I'm a bit worried about this crazy boy next door," she said. "Jumping over the wall and interfering with the rats and everything. I must talk to Charlie."

Charlie is Mr. Bateman.

I thought about Joss climbing up to the roof to meet me and in the canteen saying he was my knight in shining armor.

"He's not that bad," I said. "I mean, he's a bit weird, but I think he's all right."

"Darling Blue." She moved over to make room for me on the bed, and opened her arms for a hug. "Always so sweet."

Sweet is even worse than *sensible*.

"Everything all right at school?" She asked like she already knew the answer, because unlike Flora I have always been a model pupil. I thought about telling her the truth—about Dodi and Cressida and nobody talking to me and being invisible—but she had already fallen asleep.

I turned out the light and I lay there next to her with my head right on her shoulder, and she smelled of Diorissimo and the garden. Sometimes, when we were little, she used to lie down with us for our afternoon naps, and it felt just like this. I would have been happy to stay like that all night, but then Jas started yelling from the Babes' room that Twig was sleeping under his bed instead of on it.

"It's for my *survival training*!" roared Twig.

"It's *creepy!*" she screamed back.

"He's also naked." Flora barged into my room looking like the Living Dead with purple hair dye dripping down her neck. "No wonder she's freaking out."

And so the whole mad circus started again.

Dodi Cartwright is a Total Cow.

That is what I told Jake Lyall this afternoon when he took me to the infirmary because the cut on my forehead was bleeding.

"Technically speaking," Jake said, "Cressida is the cow, because she is the one who pulled away your chair."

"She did it to impress Dodi," I said. "And Dodi laughed."

"Dude," said Jake, "*everybody* laughed."

Once when we were in Devon after Iris died Dad took us to the sea during a storm, and he made us all stand in a line and yell as loud as we could. It was winter and with the wind and the waves crashing into the shingle and the sound of our own bellowing, we couldn't even hear each other. "Louder," Dad shouted. "Louder!" and Jas started to cry and Mum said, "David, stop," and Flora said, "This is stupid," but I went on shouting even after all the others had stopped, just me looking at this big angry sea. My voice started to crack, but I didn't move until the spray started flying up almost as high as the waves and Mum dragged me off the beach.

That is where I would like to be in moments like today, when Cressida pulls away my chair and everybody laughs even though I'm bleeding and Anthea Foundry is too dumb to realize what has happened and nobody stands up for me.

Jake and I were friends at Saint Swithins. Once, when we were eight, he tried to kiss me behind the toilets. I didn't let him. In fact, I ran away screaming, but still. It ought to count for something.

"Blue?" said Jake. "You all right?"

Jake looked worried, like he thought I might burst into tears or something, and I realized that my front teeth were clamped together, which makes my chin stick out like I'm about to cry or lose my temper.

"Dude, I know you're cross with me." Jake looked really sorry, and a tiny bit ashamed, which was good, but not good enough.

"Just shut up, Jake," I started to say, except suddenly Jake wasn't actually there anymore.

"I'll take over," said Joss. And just like that we were alone together.

Joss took one look at my forehead and announced that what I needed wasn't the infirmary at all but to get out of school. He marched me across the playground and out through the gate without anyone batting an eye.

"The secret to life," he announced, "is to do things with confidence."

I don't drink coffee but he didn't give me a choice. We went to Home Sweet Home, where I went for lunch on the first day of term, and while I was in the bathroom cleaning up my cut he ordered cappuccinos and chocolate fridge cake. While he ate he made me tell him what happened.

"But why?" he asked when I finished. "Why did she pull away the chair?"

I didn't answer. Joss leaned forward. His eyes are light brown with these little flecks of gold. He smiled and for a moment I was tempted to explain, I really was, but then I shook my head because it's too painful and complicated and I honestly wouldn't know where to start.

"You know, you would get along much better with people if you actually talked," he said.

"But I don't want to," I said.

"Fair enough." Joss finished his cake and started on mine. "Tell me about your family instead. Start with your name. Who the hell is called Blue anyway?"

I told him about the parents and how they had given us all flower names to remember the good old days when they pretended to be hippies at Glastonbury, and how Flora and Jas loved theirs but that I thought Bluebell was better suited to a cow. Joss laughed at that, which was a nice feeling because I can't remember anyone *ever* finding me funny. I told him that Twig hated that his real name was Jonathan and chose his nickname to be more like the rest of us, and that Twig might seem silly but that it was a lot better than his first choice, which was Acorn. Joss laughed again, and then he asked loads more questions, like why is Flora's hair pink, and what do I film with my camera, and who are my favorite directors, and if my life was a movie which one would it be, and Cressida Taylor apart how do I like Clarendon Free School and could he have my e-mail address?

We talked for ages. We didn't go back to school. Joss said I might have a concussion, and it would be better to go home. I have never blown off school before, and I rather liked it. We walked through the park and messed around on the swings. It's colder now the summer's gone. It's still light enough to stay out in the afternoon but the leaves are autumn colored, and when Joss pushed me the wind on my face smelled like bonfires. I got home just before Flora. Joss walked me around and told Zoran he'd brought me home because I wasn't well.

"I'll sort it with school," he whispered as he left.

"How?" I whispered back.

He didn't say anything, but tapped the side of his nose with his finger and winked. Normally I hate it when people do that, but the way he did it made me laugh.

"Why are you looking at me like that?" I asked Zoran when Joss had gone.

"I am not looking at you," said Zoran. "Or if I am it is completely accidental."

"I haven't done anything wrong," I said.

"Define *wrong*," said Zoran.

I don't *know* if the house has changed since Iris died, or if I just think it has.

My new room, which we used to think was so tiny, doesn't feel small to me anymore at all. It feels just the right size but our old room, which used to feel so cramped when there were two of us in it because Iris was the messiest person in the history of messy people, now feels huge. And the kitchen table feels wrong if there aren't seven people sitting at it, and it doesn't help if Zoran is here or Grandma or Flora's friends or anyone else to make up the numbers, because the seventh person is supposed to have dark brown eyes and mousy hair cut in a bob like mine, and apart from the fact that she doesn't wear glasses and always has a bandanna around her neck she is supposed to look just like me.

We were in Devon on the first anniversary of Iris's death. Christmas Eve. Mum and Dad bundled us out of bed and we drove to the beach, and as the sun came up we threw her ashes over the sea and watched them scatter on the wind.

For the second anniversary, we went to Midnight Mass. Church is not something our family does much, except for Mum, who when she is here goes at odd times like Tuesday night or very early on Sunday morning. But for the second anniversary, Mum insisted. She said it was important to ask

God to please look after Iris in heaven. Dad said he would only go to give God a piece of his mind, but when he got to church he lit his candle alongside the rest of us, and by the time we had lit one candle each for Iris, and then for one another, and Jas and Twig had lit a lot of random ones for everyone from the rats to their teachers, there was a whole table of candles blazing just for us. The choir was singing "Silent Night," and Dad said it was corny beyond his wildest dreams, but he was crying.

On December third it will be three years since Iris's accident, and on Christmas Eve it will be three years since she died. Sometimes I think I'm the only person who actually remembers this.

I miss her.

SUNDAY, OCTOBER 2 (VERY, VERY LATE AT NIGHT)

Mum and Dad were both away this weekend and even though the rain stopped it was still gray and Flora was in a bad mood so Zoran decided we should watch *War and Peace* to cheer her up. In Russian.

"How could that possibly cheer me up?" demanded Flora.

"The ballroom scenes are beautiful," said Zoran. "And one of the battle scenes lasts forty-five minutes."

"God!" cried Flora. Twig screamed "I've been shot!" and lay convulsing on the floor until Zoran announced it was time for more sausages.

The Russian version of *War and Peace* has four parts and a combined running time of seven hours. What with meals and Flora's rehearsal for the Christmas Extravaganza of Fairy Tales and the Babes' karate class, it took us most of the weekend to get through it, by which time Jas was crying nonstop because so many people were dead, Twig had piled all his bedroom furniture in the middle of the room to build a fort, I had finished my homework for what felt like the rest of term, and Flora had entered a trance.

"I might learn Russian," she told Zoran as she went up to bed.

"I knew you'd like it," he said.

"I hated it," she assured him. "It was the worst experience of my life. But there were times when they were talking that I thought it actually sounded quite pretty, and I realized I rather loved it, too."

Zoran looked delighted.

"She said she hated it," I reminded him.

"Not all of it," he said.

He started watching the whole thing again once we had gone upstairs. I heard him because I was checking my e-mails in Dad's study just above the den. Flora threw the WiFi router away after our last Skype session with Mum, when she told her that *visual telecommunication is no substitute for proper mothering.* There is an ADSL modem in the study so that is where we have to go for e-mails or the Internet until one of our wandering parents or Zoran gets a new router installed. Which is unlikely to happen any time soon.

There was one e-mail from Mum addressed to all of us, saying she wishes she was with us and complaining how noisy it is in New York, and there was the usual stuff you get just by having an e-mail account from people trying to sell you things, and buried among those a weird one from Dad asking had we seen the film *King Arthur—The Untold True Story*, and also had we seen *A Knight's Tale* and what did we think of them both even though they are quite different.

"Yes, we have seen *A Knight's Tale* loads of times," I wrote to Dad. "It's very funny. We haven't seen *King Arthur*, but I have just googled it and it is full of battle scenes and quite frankly I've had enough of those to last me a lifetime."

A chat box popped up in gmail while I was writing to Dad, which was a shock because nobody ever chats with me, and it was from Joss, saying *good you're there I'm coming over.* Not, *I'm bored and could I come over,* or *I'm sorry it's ten o'clock at night and I know that's kind of late and would it disturb you if I came over.* Just, *I'm coming over.*

It took me a while to get the hang of the chat box thing, and by the time I thought of something to say and typed

61

how do you know I'm here, I could be anywhere Joss had sent me an e-mail from his iPhone saying he was at my bedroom window.

"This girl who pulled away your chair," he said when I got back to my room, "tell me about her."

At first we sat like we did the first time he came, with him on the roof and me just inside the window, but it got too uncomfortable once I started talking, because he had to lean forward with his head sticking into the room saying *What? What?* and I had to whisper really loudly, which hurt my throat. So then I climbed out, dragging my duvet with me, and we laid it out sideways and both lay on it, with the end wrapped up and over me because I was cold in my pajamas, and I was able to whisper normally.

"That's better," said Joss. "Now start again from the beginning."

I didn't want to talk. I lay next to him and closed my eyes and listened to London rumble, and a little part of me deep inside just marveled at what I was doing.

"Blue?"

"It's complicated."

I turned on my side to look at him and realized that he wasn't going to give up, so I told him what I told Jake.

"Cressida's not really the problem," I said. "I mean she's horrible, but she's only trying to impress Dodi."

"Who is?"

"Her best friend." I swallowed. "Who used to be mine."

"Ah," said Joss. "I see."

No, I thought. *You don't. You really, really don't.*

"So what happened?" asked Joss.

"Nothing," I lied. "We just fell out." And then we were quiet again for a while.

"You don't have to just take it, you know," he said. "You can stand up for yourself."

"I don't think I know how to," I said.

"We'll think of something. I'll help you. I'm very good at defending myself."

A picture came into my head of Graham Lewis sprawled on the canteen floor covered in chips.

"I suppose you are," I said.

Joss propped himself up on one elbow and smiled down at me.

"I'm going to save you," he said. "Clearly, that's why I've been sent to London."

"Why *were* you sent to London?" I asked. "I mean, really?"

Joss rolled his eyes. "I wasn't given a choice."

I rolled my eyes back. "What about standing up for yourself?"

"Questions, questions . . ." All of a sudden he was on his feet, with his beanie pulled back down, getting ready to go.

"Time for bed," he said. "Night night, gorgeous." He blew me a kiss and then he was gone.

I am trying not to think about the fact that Joss Bateman blew me a kiss or that he called me gorgeous.

Gorgeous, used the way he used it, is just a word at the end of a sentence.

MONDAY, OCTOBER 3

Joss is not as good at sorting things with school as he claims to be. This morning at break I had to go to the headmaster (Call Me God)'s office to explain how I came to disappear from school halfway through Friday afternoon.

"I didn't feel well," I mumbled.

"Your classmate Mr. Lyall says he left you with the nurse. And yet the nurse says she never saw you."

"It's not Jake's fault," I said.

God gave me that look teachers give you when they know that short of using physical torture they're not going to get any more out of you.

"I am Very Disappointed in You, Bluebell Gadsby," he said (he always uses capital letters when he is giving a lecture). "I like to think of you as the Sensible One of your Family. I hope this is not the Beginning of a Slippery Slope."

On the way out I bumped into Flora, waiting for her weekly argument with God about her appearance.

"What are *you* doing here?" she cried.

She was furious when I explained. Flora is not nearly as rebellious as she looks. She may like to shock people with her bright hair and her weird outfits, she may have a gazillion friends and always be right at the glittering center of a very big crowd, but she could be as small and mousy and bespectacled as me for all the rules she actually breaks.

"You can't just blow off school like that!" she ranted at me. "What if Mum and Dad found out?"

"Oh, get lost, Flora," I said at last, and she just gaped at me because like everybody else she is just not used to me answering back.

"What?"

"I said, get lost." I marched off, leaving her watching me with her mouth hanging open, even though God was shouting at her to come into his office.

I stood up for myself.

And it felt good.

FRIDAY, OCTOBER 7

Twig and Jas announced this morning that they wanted to walk to school on their own. Zoran said no, that one of his Express Duties was to take them to school and what would Mum say if she found out something had happened to them?

"At the rate she's going," said Flora, "she will probably never know."

Mum is in New York this week, and Flora's hair now has scarlet streaks.

Zoran said, "That's not fair; your mother loves you very much," and then when Flora said, "Ha!" he added that it didn't suit her to sound so sour, and she said that was rich coming from him and then they started to argue about which of them had the most reason to be bitter about their parents. Which is Zoran, obviously, because even though we are practically orphans Mum told us that his parents actually *are* dead. While they were fighting, I watched Twig and Jas slip out of the house and head off toward school, way earlier than they normally would, but I guess they just saw their chance and took it. Zoran was furious when he realized they had gone. Flora hasn't laughed so hard in ages.

I hadn't seen Joss all week until this evening, not to talk to I mean, but then he came around again tonight, climbing onto the roof as usual. It was cold and I thought of asking him in, but then I worried someone would hear so I climbed out instead.

"I've been thinking," he said. "This Dodi cow. We have to take her down."

"Um," I said.

Joss laughed. "Just give me the dirt on her," he said, "and you will have sweet revenge."

"Dirt?" I said.

"There must be *something*," said Joss. "Some murky secret from her past. Something she's scared of."

"Dodi, scared?" Dodi might look like Barbie, all blond hair and sparkly clothes, but underneath she's tough. Last year when we went rappelling on our school trip, she was the first one to go over the edge, and then she stood at the bottom laughing at anyone who said they were scared of heights.

"I think actually most people are a little afraid of *her*," I said.

"You're not trying," Joss scolded.

He looked so earnest. The sky behind him was dark tonight, not orange. That happens sometimes, I've noticed. Zoran cut the lawn this afternoon—he says it will be the last time this year—and the air was sharp with the smell of grass. Joss was in shadows but I could see his profile, his turned up nose and hair falling in his eyes. He was waiting for an answer.

I thought, maybe I should tell him why it's complicated.

Instead, I told him what he needed to know.

THE FILM DIARIES OF BLUEBELL GADSBY
SCENE SEVEN (TRANSCRIPT)
THE FALL OF DODI CARTWRIGHT

DAYTIME. CLASS 8A'S FORM ROOM, VIEWED FROM
BENEATH THE DESK WHERE CAMERAMAN (BLUE)
IS FILMING IN SECRET. AFTERNOON, THE BREAK
IN THE MIDDLE OF DOUBLE FRENCH.

MADAME GILBERT has just left the room and will not
return for eight and a half minutes, the time it takes
her to scurry to the staff room and down a double
espresso. Camera pans slowly, taking in linoleum floor,
the underside of desks bristling with gum, the legs of
tables, chairs, and humans before settling on the lower
half of the door just as it begins to creak open.

Picture shakes as CAMERAMAN (BLUE) retrieves
camera from beneath desk. Nobody sees her. All eyes
are turned to the door, drawn by the whir and squeak
that followed the opening creak. They expect to see
Madame Gilbert. The expressions on their faces range
from anticipation (HATTIE VERNEY, class know-it-

all) to torpor (JAKE LYALL, who is almost asleep), to indifference (almost everybody else), but they change when they see who the newcomer is. Jake wakes up and begins to laugh. Hattie is horrified. They both look incredulous. All other faces reflect a combination of the above. For sitting in the doorway, strapped into a remote-controlled model of a Jaguar XK120 SE DHC convertible, is a large white rat.

THE CLASS holds its collective breath, knowing that to attract attention to itself now would be fatal to their enjoyment of what is to come. THE GREAT WHITE RAT (for it is he) sits in the driver's seat, plotting his escape strategy. The Jaguar's whirring increases to a low scream, and then both it and its rodent passenger are on the move.

Camera shakes as the class erupts. Girls scream. Boys cheer. Everybody laughs. The Great White Rat struggles against the bonds which shackle him, in the form of an orange knitted tie. The car veers a bit from left to right, as if operated by someone who can't quite see what he is doing. Door creaks again. Camera pans briefly left, JOSS steps into door frame from corridor where he has been hiding, holding the remote control. Nobody turns to look at him, but the car now moves

in a straight line toward the only silent person in the
room who isn't holding a video camera.

> DODI
> (very pale, through clenched teeth)
> Get lost, ratty.

> JAWS THE GREAT WHITE RAT
> *Eeeeeeeek!*

> JAKE
> (yelling, as if teachers didn't exist)
> HERE COME ANOTHER TWO!

Camera, no longer bothering to hide, whips back to
the door. BETSY and PETAL, in Twig's battered Aston
Martin and a brand-new Alfa Romeo, are motoring into
the room and also making a beeline for DODI. They
come to a halt a foot away from her, all three cars
fanned out in a semicircle.

> DODI
> (looking green)
> This is so not funny.

BETSY, PETAL, and JAWS THE GREAT WHITE RAT
(squirming and gnawing at the Ties Which Bind
Them)
Eek! Squeak! Eek, eek, eek!

DODI
I'm getting out of here.

She notices Blue, who is still filming.

DODI, (cont.)
(attempting a sneer)
What, you thought I'd be scared?

Blue does not answer but continues to film (bravely).
Dodi curls her lip, grabs her schoolbag with every appearance of bravado, opens it to toss in her French
book, and complete dramatic exit.

DODI, (cont., again)
AGGGHHHH!

CASPAR (one of the male baby rats) shoots out of the
bag, panics, runs up Dodi's arm and onto her head
to which he clings, quivering and keening. The class
roars. Dodi bursts into tears and sinks sobbing to

the ground. The race cars rev their engines, rocking back and forth. Betsy (or is it Petal) breaks loose of the Aston Martin and shoots through a tangle of legs, causing more screams and hysterical laughter. A cheering crowd has gathered by the door. Nobody notices when Madame Gilbert returns, shouting in French, or when GOD turns up, waving detention slips, or when Joss slips in wearing a satisfied grin. The pandemonium only subsides when FLORA streaks into the room, screaming blue murder and brandishing a lacrosse stick.

FLORA
(landing lacrosse stick neatly over Petal, or maybe Betsy)
I knew it! I knew they were ours as soon as I heard there were rats!

GOD
What do you mean, yours? Flora Gadsby, are these your rats?

FLORA
(to Joss, still screaming)
What on earth do you think you're doing?

JOSS
(calmly)
I was delivering justice.

FLORA
(shoveling rats into her messenger bag)
Justice! Ha!

GOD
I demand you answer my question!

JOSS
(nobly)
I claim full responsibility, sir.

MADAME GILBERT
(hysterically)
Quel horrible garçon! Never would such a thing
happen in France.

FLORA
(rudely)
For God's sake, you eat *frogs' legs!*

GOD
Miss Gadsby, you are in detention! Mr. Bateman,

so are you! (*Spots Blue, who is still filming*) And you too, Bluebell Gadsby! In fact, this whole class is in detention! I will not have rodents in my school or chaos in my classrooms! (*Spots Dodi, still cowering on the floor*). Stand up, Miss Cartwright! Miss Cartwright! You are not a child.

Dodi Cartwright struggles slowly to her feet. Those closest to her wrinkle their noses. They look puzzled until, slowly, they begin to understand.

Dodi Cartwright has a large damp patch on the back of her skirt and a yellow puddle at her feet.

Camera goes off with a satisfied click.

FRIDAY, OCTOBER 21

They went nuts at home.

"What a thoroughly irresponsible thing to do!" scolded Zoran.

"Poor Jaws! Poor Caspar! Poor Betsy and Petal!" cried Jas.

"You could have lost them! You could have killed them! You could have broken the cars!" shouted Twig.

"To say nothing of that poor girl, being publicly humiliated! You should be ashamed of yourself, Blue," said Zoran, but I could see that he was trying not to laugh.

And here's the thing. They all screamed at me when I got home, and Zoran is still being all disapproving, but they made me play the video. And then after I'd played it, they made me play it again. And again. And each time, it became a little bit less about cruelty to Dodi and the rats and a lot more about animal stardom.

"Doesn't Betsy look cute in the Alfa Romeo!" cooed Jas.

"And Caspar!" cried Twig. "Isn't he brave?"

"That woman is wrong and completely discriminatory," said Zoran. "I'm sure exactly the same thing happens in French classrooms."

"Not *exactly* the same thing," said Flora. "Surely never *exactly* the same thing. This is unique." And they all stared at me like they couldn't believe it was me who had done it.

Later, when the Babes had gone to bed, Flora told Zoran everything Joss had told her about Dodi and Cressida during detention, when they were supposed to be working on a math assignment but were actually having a fierce whispered argument in the back of the classroom with the rats chewing everything in Flora's messenger bag (the one she has customized by turning all the flowers into skulls). It was almost dark by the time they let us out of school. We all walked home together and Flora apologized for not realizing what a cow Dodi was being to me.

"I knew you weren't friends anymore," she said. "But I didn't realize she was actually being horrible."

"You must have noticed Blue was unhappy," said Joss.

"No more than usual," said Flora, but she said it nicely, and she took my hand and squeezed it, which is as close to "sorry" as you get from Flora.

"I wish you'd come to me," she said.

"Joss found out first."

"Thank you, Joss," said Flora stiffly. "For looking after my sister."

"Anytime," said Joss. Flora sniffed and said this didn't mean she approved of cruelty to animals.

"I wish you'd told me, too," said Zoran.

"I will next time," I promised as I went up to bed, because it seemed to be what he wanted to hear. I yawned. Flora and Zoran stood together at the bottom of the stairs, looking concerned, but I left them to it. I got undressed and into bed, and now I am lying here, thinking about what Zoran said about feeling ashamed of myself.

Dodi's house backs onto a huge communal garden, and when Mum said we were old enough to walk there on our own, we *lived* there. We went there every day after school through all of that last summer term, and we played there for hours, long complicated pretend games invented by Iris. Dodi's mum brought our tea out, and we were so hungry but having so much fun that we ate it as we played.

Until the Mouse Picnic.

The picnic when, for once, we were playing so hard we forgot about tea, and a field mouse—a teeny-weeny field mouse—scampered out of the undergrowth to nibble at a jam sandwich.

Iris saw it first. She stopped running and she whispered, "Oh, oh, oh" like it was the sweetest, most important thing she had ever seen in her entire life, and she tiptoed toward it.

I stood still and watched. The mouse looked up and sniffed. Its whiskers twitched, but it really liked that sandwich and Iris walked so softly, so softly . . . She untied her bandanna—she told me later that was going to catch the mouse with it.

"And I would have, too," she complained, "if it hadn't been for Dodi."

Dodi didn't think the mouse was sweet. She didn't stop, or say "oh, oh, oh," or watch with bated breath.

Dodi saw the mouse, screamed, and fainted dead away.

I had forgotten all about it until Joss asked. I'm worried that I'm starting to forget lots of things about Iris too. Because that story is as much about Iris as it is about Dodi.

Really, I suppose, it is about the three of us, and how we used to be.

Back when we were friends Dodi wore glasses just like mine, little wire-framed ones, which made her look a bit mad because one of her ears is higher than the other so they were always crooked, plus her mum always made her wear her hair in braids, which made the mad crooked thing worse. Now she's all glamorous with contact lenses and her hair all layered, and the point is Zoran doesn't have to put up with her meanness. He doesn't spend his days being miserable and lonely or having chairs pulled out from under him.

Good things happened today. Really good things.

People whispering "nice one, Blue" in detention, Jake high-fiving me as we all left. It's like a spell has been broken. Suddenly I'm visible again, and I like it.

I don't care what Zoran says. Today was absolutely perfect.

SATURDAY, OCTOBER 22 (EARLY EVENING)

Zoran had a long conversation with Mr. Bateman this morning in the front garden. He said that Mr. Bateman had come to apologize for Joss's part in what he calls *the great rat debacle*, and said that Joss had a history of what he called "unruly behavior."

"He saved me," I said, and Zoran said, "even so" and sniffed.

Zoran is very traditional.

Joss came around when the others were all out, Flora at a rehearsal and Zoran at karate with the Babes. He said it was to bring stuff back, like rat food and a water bottle and the bag he took them to school in, but then he hovered on the doorstep sort of looking over my shoulder until I asked him in.

It was strange being alone in the house with him. Very different from talking on the roof when everyone was asleep. I made tea, and he slumped down at the kitchen counter to drink it.

"I've been grounded," he said.

"Because of yesterday?" I asked.

"Yeah." Joss pulled a face. "And I was supposed to be going home today. One of my friends is having a party."

"I'm sorry," I stammered.

"Don't be silly!" He smiled and his whole face lit up, like the party didn't matter and he'd already forgotten about it. "It was totally worth it. The look on God's face when he realized she'd wet herself!"

I felt a twinge of guilt at that, but Joss was grinning all over his face now and it was impossible not to grin back, and then before I could say anything Zoran and the Babes were piling into the house with Flora right behind them, and it was impossible to get a word in edgeways.

"How could you do it?" cried Jas, meaning how could Joss be so cruel to the rats. She has decided she really doesn't like him, even though she has never actually spoken to him.

79

"How *did* you do it?" asked Twig.

"Don't encourage him," said Flora.

"But I really want to know!"

They all crowded around him except Zoran, and Joss looked as relaxed as if he was in his own home surrounded by his oldest friends. "We did loads of planning," he said. "But they're obviously very well trained."

"I always said they enjoyed the car rides," nodded Twig. "Didn't I, Zoran? And you never believed me."

"I'm going to make lunch," said Zoran.

I invited Joss to eat with us, but he said he couldn't because he was theoretically grounded for the rest of his life and had to get back.

"There wasn't enough food anyway," said Zoran when he had gone.

Joss texted me as soon as he got back to say his grandparents had gone out and did I want to come and watch a movie. Flora came with me. She said Joss might have saved me from Dodi's bullying but she didn't trust him farther than she could throw a cat.

"Which is also cruel to animals," I told her. "And you sound like Zoran. I don't think he likes Joss either."

"Zoran is not entirely devoid of sense," said Flora.

She decided we should watch *Twilight*.

"But he's a boy," I said, and she said duh, of course, and that this was a test.

"He'll hate it!"

"It's *why* he hates it that's important."

I haven't been inside Mr. and Mrs. Bateman's house for ages. They used to have a party every Christmas but they stopped a few years ago, Dad says because a lot of their friends died or moved away and they found they didn't really like the people who were left. Not even us, he says, and no wonder because we are so noisy, what with Flora's music and everybody shouting all the time. So now there are no parties, and at Christmas they just give us jars of homemade marmalade, but their house hasn't changed a bit.

It should be exactly like ours, but it isn't. I mean the layout is the same, but our house feels quite cool and dark and echoey because the floor in the hall is these old marble tiles, and in the other rooms it's all wood Mum has painted black to show off the carpets they bought in Anatolia when they went backpacking there with Flora when she was a baby. We have to stuff cushions and scarves on our windows to stop them from rattling when it's windy, and we have these massive thick curtains because of the drafts, royal blue velvet with random crimson flowers Mum started embroidering then gave up. Joss's grandparents' house is very quiet and warm, because they have pale green carpet everywhere and these new windows that don't let in drafts. All their furniture matches. Mr. and Mrs. Bateman have gray hair and wear beige cardigans and do a lot of gardening. It seems quite extraordinary to me that Joss is their grandson.

Joss passed the *Twilight* test. He laughed out loud at the sparkly vampire bit and he squirmed through all the love scenes, but he liked the camera work and he thought Victoria, the beautiful evil she vampire, was awesome.

"The other one, the little female vampire, she was cool, too," he said when it was finished.

"Alice," said Flora. "I love her hair."

"I don't know about that," said Joss, "but I liked the way she ripped that psycho vampire's head off at the end."

Flora looked almost approving, but then she frowned and asked him what he thought about the film's antifeminist message and the way it reinforces gender stereotypes. Only Flora can ask questions like that and not sound like a nerd.

"I didn't," said Joss. "Think about it, I mean."

"The weak and feeble woman, the strong dominant male!" cried Flora.

"I thought women liked dangerous men," said Joss, and Flora went pink. And then I asked Joss if he wanted to see the footage from yesterday and he said, "Hell, yeah!" and we all huddled up on the sofa to watch it and Joss laughed and laughed.

"It's brilliant!" he said. "And doubly amazing seeing as you were filming in secret."

"It wasn't very secret by the end."

"Blue's always filming stuff," grumbled Flora, like what she meant was "the amount of filming she does she bloody well should be good."

"Well it shows." Joss smiled at me and Flora's grumbling didn't matter so much. And then we all sat on the sofa a bit more and Joss flipped through other things I had filmed before. He laughed at the one of himself climbing over our garden wall, and then he asked Flora if she'd like a beer and she said no, she doesn't drink.

I said I'd like a beer and Joss roared with laughter and hugged me, but Flora ignored us.

"We have to go," she said, and I have never heard her sound so prim. "We're having dinner with our parents."

"Woo-hoo," said Joss.

Flora went pink again.

"Come on, Blue," she said. "We're going home."

I wriggled out from under Joss's arm.

"You could come, too," I told him.

"I'm not sure I could bear the excitement," he whispered.

"You've got a crush on him," said Flora on the way home.

"I do not!" I told her.

"Yes, you do. You're falling for him big-time."

"We're *friends*!"

"Well I don't think you should hang out with him," said Flora. "He has a very dodgy attitude toward women."

"Just because he didn't agree with you about gender stereotypes," I mumbled, but we were already home and she swept into the house without listening to me.

People who think that being friends with a boy is the same thing as having a crush really annoy me.

And so now here we all are, waiting for the parents. We set the table, and Jas decorated it with some late roses from the garden and ivy which she trailed around the plates. Flora got out Mum's recipe books and she and Zoran are learning how to make chicken casserole and dumplings, because Flora has said she will scream if she ever so much as sees another sausage. They are listening to the Rolling Stones as they cook and, even though Flora says the Stones are ancient, she is singing along just as loudly as Zoran. Dad has called from Paddington and Mum has called from Heathrow and they are both on their way home. The Babes are dancing around the kitchen, and I am going to join them.

Dinner was hopeless. I mean properly hopeless, as in all the hopes we had that it was going to be a lovely evening were dashed almost immediately. If I had filmed it, which I didn't because Flora wouldn't let me, it would have gone something like this (after everyone had kissed, and Mum had exclaimed over the table decorations, and Dad had poured wine for him and Mum and Zoran, and we had all started to eat and gotten over the surprise that dinner was actually nice, and Jas had told the parents all about Friday and the rats):

MOTHER
(turning wistfully to Blue)
Darling, I wish I had known all this was going on at school.

BLUE
(wimping out on what she really wants to say)
That's all right, Mum.

FLORA
(not wimping out of what Blue really wants to say)
How could you possibly have known since you're never here?

ZORAN

Flora, I don't think that's very fair to your mother.

FLORA

(snarling)

Shut up, Zoran.

MOTHER

Darling, please don't speak to Zoran like that.
He's quite right. I am not the only parent around
this table who is often absent.

FATHER

(looking startled)

Don't bring me into this.

FLORA

Why on earth not?

MOTHER

I Skype every day! Or at least I did, until the
connection stopped working.

FATHER

How can the connection not be working? I only
just installed it!

MOTHER
YOUR FATHER DIDN'T EVEN KNOW THE
CONNECTION WAS BROKEN!!!

FLORA
You're both behaving like children.

TWIG
I want to have my birthday party at the Natural
History Museum.

Which at least stopped the Battle of the Skype Connection, but started another one about What Parents Should or Shouldn't Be Prepared to Do for Their Children's Birthdays. Twig's friend Jason had a birthday sleepover party at the Science Museum last weekend, and now Twig wants to do the same thing in the Natural History Museum for his birthday next month, because ever since our trip there with Zoran it is his favorite museum.

"But *where* do you sleep?" asked Mum.

"Under the *Diplodocus*," said Twig.

"That doesn't sound very comfortable."

"It's not supposed to be comfortable," said Twig. "In fact, you're not really supposed to sleep. They take you around the whole museum by torchlight and you play games."

"What, all night?"

"At Jason's party," said Twig, "we went to bed at half-past four in the morning. Or rather, we got into our sleeping bags. We didn't have beds, or even mattresses. I would also like a sleeping bag."

"We have lots of sleeping bags, son," said Dad. "From our old backpacking days." He sort of grinned at Mum but she ignored him.

"I don't think I can do all-night parties," she told Twig. "Not while I'm living in different time zones."

That was when Zoran bundled Flora and me away from the table and made us do the washing up.

"But you sleep *right underneath the dinosaur!*" Twig began to cry, and Flora balled her fists in the soapy water. "He's *one hundred and fifty million years old!*"

"Get the ice cream out of the freezer," Zoran told me. He took Flora by the shoulders.

"I can't stand them," she whimpered. "I mean it. I hate them."

"Calm down," said Zoran.

There's only one thing that stops Jas from crying, and that's if Twig beats her to it. "You take us," she ordered Dad. "If she's too tired."

"I, um, well," said Dad. "I've been meaning to tell you, son. I'm going to be a bit tied up for your birthday."

Flora walked out, slamming the door.

Nobody ate the ice cream.

Dad has gone again, after another argument, this time over Christmas. Mum, who has now agreed to sleeping with dinosaurs, tried to make up for the fact that she ever hesitated by suggesting that we all spend Christmas in New York, where she has a friend who can lend us her apartment, and the plane tickets would be our present. Even Flora was excited. Mum asked me if I thought it would be good to get away this Christmas, and even though I would rather be at home, I said yes because it was so lovely to see her smile. And then she looked at Dad and said, *"What now, David?"* And he looked sheepish and she sighed and said, *"Oh for heaven's sake, not that again."* Because Dad is terrified of flying and has vowed that he will never set foot on an airplane "unless he absolutely has to."

"Well," said Flora, "you absolutely have to now."

"I don't see why your mother can't come home for Christmas," said Dad, and they argued until he left.

Mum went to bed straight after dinner. We all pretended to go at the same time as her, but then snuck into Flora's room.

"Are they going to get divorced?" Jas curled up against Flora in her bed with the covers pulled over them. I sat on the sheepskin rug on the floor with Twig.

"Possibly," said Flora.

"What will happen?" asked Jas.

"They'll live in separate houses and never see each other," said Twig.

"So no change, then," said Flora.

"Jason lives half with his mum and half with his dad," said Twig. "Do you think we'll have to do that?"

"Live in *China*?" said Jas. "In *New York*? In *Warwick*?"

"There is no way I'm moving to Warwick," said Flora.

"We should run away," said Twig. "That would show them."

"Show them what?" I asked, and Twig admitted he didn't know.

MONDAY, OCTOBER 24

What with one thing and another, we had all almost forgotten about the incident with the rats, except Zoran.

"You have to make it count," he said this morning. "Otherwise it will have been no more than a prank."

"She deserved it!" I protested, but Zoran was on a roll.

"You must show that you are better than her. You must put a stop to it, before she retaliates. Violence only begets violence."

"It's not a blooming war, Zoran," said Flora.

They all cheered when I came into class this morning. Jake Lyall had woken up long enough to lead them, standing on the teacher's desk with Tom Myers and Colin Morgan. Then Cressida asked if I wanted to sit next to her. Everyone pretended not to notice when Dodi came in, just a few seconds before Mr. Math.

They ignored her all day. I thought they would tease her. I even imagined myself making Zoran proud and telling them to *stop* teasing her. But it was like the enormity of what she had done—peeing all over the classroom floor— was too much for them to take in. So they did what they always do when they don't know how to behave with someone. They just pretended she wasn't there. And I guess Dodi knows the score because she didn't even try to talk to them. She walked in calmly in her tightest skinny jeans with violet All Stars and a pink batwing sweater, and when she saw what was happening she just went blank, and ate lunch alone, like she knew this was always coming to her even though she had ruled the class for the past year. It was actually quite impressive.

Dodi kept up her dignified silence until the end of the day, when we were the last two to leave Art. This term we are working on environmental catastrophe, and I am making an anti–oil spill collage with a sun shaped like the BP logo and dolphins made of silver foil dipped in black paint. I stayed behind because I'm making the sea out of ring pulls, which is much more time-consuming than I thought it would be. Dodi had finished her project but hung around for ages, watching me. I tried to ignore her, and then suddenly she said, "I'm not surprised you hate me."

I didn't know what to say, so I went on ignoring her and focused like mad on my ring pulls, and then Mr. Watkins, who is teaching us Art this term, came back in and told us he had to lock up, and I started to clean up.

Dodi followed me out of the art room.

"Do you remember how cross Iris used to be if she had to wait for us?" she said as we walked out onto the playground. "Even though she was always late for everything?"

At Iris's funeral, when the curtain fell over her coffin at the crematorium, I didn't realize it wouldn't be coming back. That is the only time I have cried in public since she died. Literally. Nobody has ever seen me cry since then, but when Dodi said that about her always being late, my eyes started to sting.

"Don't," I said. "Don't you dare talk about Iris."

For a moment I thought she was going to cry, too, but I guess Dodi still has her pride. We stared at each other, and part of me wished she *would* say something, but after a while she just turned around and marched off. For a moment I was sorry. I almost called out for her to wait, but then I remembered how horrible she has become and I just couldn't.

On the way home tonight, Joss swiped a Kit Kat from

the corner shop. He just asked me, "What's your favorite chocolate," and then he went in to Mr. Patel's and slipped it into his pocket and came out and gave it to me.

"To cheer you up," he said, and then he added, "I don't have any money" because I think I must have looked a bit shocked.

"I'll buy two tomorrow," he said. "To make up for stealing today. I'll give him a quid and tell him to keep the change. Just, right now you look like you need chocolate."

I think Iris would have liked Joss. One time, when we were little, she stole all of Flora's Halloween candy and gave it to a girl in our class whose parents wouldn't let her go trick-or-treating.

"Poor Mabel without any sweets," she said. "And anyway, Flora is breaking out."

Joss nicked a bar of my Kit Kat and swallowed it in two bites. "Just call me Robin Hood," he grinned.

Iris would definitely have liked Joss.

THURSDAY, OCTOBER 27

Mum is staying home all of this week. On Monday she gave Zoran a long list of shopping to do, with masses of fruit and vegetables and whole grain cereals and absolutely no sausages, and she has made dinner for us every single evening. She also helps us with our homework while she cooks, and when we go to bed she comes in to each of our rooms in turn and sits on the end of our bed to talk.

"She could get an Oscar for playing Perfect Mum," Flora grumbled. Flora is mad because Mum won't let us stay in London with Zoran for half term next week and is insisting that we go to Grandma's.

"What is the point of having an au pair if he doesn't look after us?" she shouted at Mum, and Mum said even au pairs need a break and anyway we always go to Grandma's for half term.

"I'm sixteen," Flora said. "I'll die of boredom in Devon," and then when Mum said it would be a good chance for her to catch up on her homework, Flora ran out of the room screaming.

Mum has told Bütylicious that she can't travel this week, and what's more that she has to leave the office by seven o'clock at the latest, except yesterday and today when she told them she was going to the doctor and the dentist when in fact she was picking Jas and Twig up from school.

"It's easier to lie," she explained.

She was sitting on my bed and she looked so pretty in her pin-striped pencil skirt and gray silk blouse and cardigan. She was wearing her little tortoiseshell glasses on the end of her nose and the fluffy slippers Flora and I gave her for Christmas last year. I don't think she has any idea we all overheard her argument with Dad, the one where she told him she deserved a life and didn't want to be stuck at home with us.

"Do you actually like your job?" I asked.

Mum's face always goes completely still when she doesn't want to answer a question. "Funny little Blue!" she said. "Why would I do it otherwise?"

I wanted to tell her how much I liked having her at home, but I knew it would only upset her, especially after the fight with Flora.

"What does it feel like to have a crush on someone?" I asked instead.

"Do you have a crush on someone?"

"I just want to know."

"Goodness, well it's been an awfully long time . . ." She lay down and I snuggled up next to her. "I suppose you think about it all the time; you always want to talk about your crush; you blush when you see him and your heart hammers and, if he talks to you, you can't even speak. Your knees go weak and you giggle a lot and you're terribly moody." She peered at me over the top of her glasses. "Does that sound familiar?"

"No."

"Well that's a relief."

I thought about what she had said when she had gone, and I thought about Joss. The rats, the café, the stealing chocolate. The lying out on the roof. I don't have any problem talking to Joss, in fact, I talk to him more than to anyone else in the world. I don't blush when I see him, or go weak at the knees. Joss makes me forget everything, and he makes me feel not alone.

FRIDAY, OCTOBER 28

If being sixteen means being like Flora, I never want to grow up.

On the way to school this morning, I told Joss we were going to Grandma's.

"Rats," he said. We use that word a lot now, for obvious reasons. "I was hoping we could all hang out."

I thought about Grandma's house, and how even though our parents always talk about it as *getting away* it never actually feels like that anymore.

"Maybe we can come back early," I suggested.

Which is when Flora went weird.

"Don't be absurd," she snapped. "You love it at Grandma's."

"I was only saying . . ."

"You're just trying to act cool in front of Joss."

"That's not fair!"

"Isn't it?"

We watched her storm off. My cheeks were burning, but Joss was laughing. "She's a bit mental, your sister," he said.

"I'm not trying to act cool," I said, and he laughed again.

"Course you're not. I know that."

"I do want to go to Grandma's, really. It's just . . ."

"You'll be all right." We stopped in front of our house and Joss was looking down at me, all serious and sympathetic, like he knew that I couldn't find the words to say what I was thinking.

"I'm sure you'll have fun." He reached out a hand and flicked the end of my nose. "I'll miss you, Bluebird."

Our front door was open. Inside, Flora and Zoran and the Babes were all yelling at each other.

"Yeah," I said. "I'll miss you, too."

DEVON

THE FILM DIARIES OF BLUEBELL GADSBY
SCENE EIGHT (TRANSCRIPT)
THE EXPLOITATION OF MINORS
OR, GRANDMA'S IDEA OF A HOLIDAY

DAYTIME, THOUGH GIVEN THE WEATHER, IT
COULD AS WELL BE NIGHT. A LARGE VEGETABLE
GARDEN IN THE GROUNDS OF AN OLD COUNTRY
FARMHOUSE SURROUNDED BY HILLS. RAIN.

FLORA, JASMINE, and TWIG are working in the
garden. Twig and Jasmine are raking paths. Flora is
hoeing. Until today, she had no idea what a hoe even
was, and though nobody knows exactly what she is
supposed to be doing with it, it is clear she is doing
it badly. Jasmine appears to have doubled in size, because in addition to the boots and anorak the others
all wear, she has put on *all her clothes*—two pairs of
jeans, three sweaters, a vest, a T-shirt, and a full set
of thermal underwear, as well as a fleece-lined Peru-
vian hat and a rug folded over her shoulders and tied
around her waist with string. She looks like a Siberian

peasant, a fact Flora has reminded her of three times already.

FLORA
(muttering, leaning on her hoe)
How long, dear God, how long?

JASMINE
Is it *actually* this cold in Siberia?

TWIG
You're being pathetic. This is how people used to live before supermarkets were invented.

JASMINE
I'm freezing!

TWIG
If you had to try and survive in the wild, you would die.

FLORA
(sinks to her knees, arms stretched toward the sky)
I have seen the error of my ways!

JASMINE

Plus, I'm hungry.

FLORA

(bursting into fake theatrical tears)

Merciful God, my children are starving!

GRANDMA

(appearing from nowhere, as usual)

FLORA GADSBY, THAT'S QUITE ENOUGH OF YOUR
AMATEUR DRAMATICS! AND BLUEBELL, YOU
CAN PUT AWAY THAT CAMERA. I SENT YOU OUT
HERE TO HELP YOUR BROTHER AND SISTERS,
NOT TO MAKE A RUDDY DOCUMENTARY!

TUESDAY, NOVEMBER 1

I have found the words for what I wanted to say to Joss
before we left.

The problem with Devon is that there is too much space.
In London I can manage the emptiness without Iris. I can
push it right down, fold it up like a piece of paper, over
and over so it's all scrunched up, and even though it's hard
and pointy and hurts I can keep it in one place, locked up
inside me where it doesn't get in the way. Whereas here, it's

like that piece of paper has unfolded itself, and just kept on growing and growing to fill all the space where Iris isn't.

Grandma believes in keeping us busy. She says that it is her grandmotherly duty to make us look LESS SICKLY—ALL THAT ROTTEN LONDON AIR! It has not stopped raining since we arrived, but it would take more than rain to make Grandma give up on her plans for us. So far these have included:

Day 1: twelve-mile hike into Dartmoor. Grandma gave us sandwiches, binoculars, and five pounds to buy some fudge from the Black Lion, which is the farthest point on our route. She said we couldn't cheat and bring fudge back from the village shop because the fudge from the Black Lion has a picture of the pub on it and isn't sold anywhere else.

Day 2: was yesterday, and the nineteenth-century child exploitation gardening scenario.

Day 3: is today, and was RIDING.

When we were here last summer, Grandma had a falling out with the riding stables BECAUSE THEY WOULDN'T LET US GALLOP.

"Because of the insurance," the riding stables lady said.

Grandma said this was PREPOSTEROUS and how could we learn to ride properly if we weren't allowed a bit of speed? And the riding stables lady said it wasn't her fault, it was the new health and safety laws the government had brought in, and Grandma said "ruddy health and safety."

And so now Grandma has bought two ponies, because apparently health and safety laws are different if you have your own horse. So Twig and Jas had a lesson this morning in Grandma's paddock, and this afternoon Flora and I went out onto the moor again, this time with instructions not to come back until we'd had A JOLLY GOOD GALLOP.

"I'm a little bit scared," I told Flora, because, apart from practicing a bit in the paddock yesterday and the day before, we hadn't ridden since the summer and obviously, for all the reasons I have written, we had never galloped.

Flora admitted that she was, too.

"We could pretend," I said.

"She would know," sighed Flora. "Grandma always knows. She'd be able to tell by their sweat or something."

And we both looked quite crossly at the ponies, who could probably tell we don't actually like riding because they were all frisky and shaking their heads like they were showing us they couldn't care less what we thought or wanted.

So we did gallop. The ponies didn't give us a choice. We reached the end of the stone path behind the house, where it opens up onto the moor, and they just took off and it was . . . well, it was amazing! There was this sort of surge and the ponies leaped forward, and my eyes were streaming from the wind, and the rain was whipping my cheeks, and the ponies' hooves were thundering on the moor, and everything was flashing by so fast I only caught glimpses of the river we splashed through and a stone sheepfold, a startled pheasant, a cairn. The ponies slowed down when the hill became steeper, where the ground turns brown and barren. We finally managed to make them stop and that is when I fell off. Flora said "idiot!" and then she was laughing so much she fell off, too, and we lay on our backs looking up at the sky where a bird was wheeling and calling on its own.

Flora says that if she were a horse and lost her rider, especially on Dartmoor, she would gallop away and hide and live a life free from the tyranny of men. But Grandma's ponies just wandered off to eat some grass, and I swear they barely noticed when we got back in the saddles. Grandma didn't check their sweat when we got home. She just looked pleased and told us to untack them and brush them and give them some hay and water, then come in for tea, which was crumpets and chocolate cake Jas and Twig had made with her while we were riding when they weren't OUT GATHERING STUFF TO BURN ON TOMORROW NIGHT'S BONFIRE.

Grandma has announced that tomorrow is a FREE DAY, which no doubt means more riding and hiking, and at some point we are going surfing. Winter surfing is a "treat" usually reserved for New Year's Day, but Grandma has said that we look SO peaky this year we get to do it twice. This evening, though, there was no more fresh air and no more excitement. We sat by the fire and played cards, except I actually fell asleep, and Flora told me that while I slept I kept saying "faster, faster" and that I couldn't stop smiling.

"Which makes a nice change," she said, but she looked pleased and anyway, it's true.

WEDNESDAY, NOVEMBER 2

Today it didn't stop raining and Flora said that's it, she doesn't care how much Grandma thinks e-mail rots your brain and won't allow us to use it except for emergencies, this was a total emergency.

"IN WHAT WAY, YOUNG LADY?" Grandma boomed.

Flora said, "I haven't posted for so long my friends will think I'm dead." Grandma is very up to date in many ways, but that just floored her.

My own e-mail inbox was empty. Even Mum hadn't written, I suppose because she knows we are at Grandma's and unlikely to be allowed to check. I went onto Facebook. In all the time since I set up my Facebook page (because Flora told me to), nobody except her has ever posted anything on my wall or asked to be my friend, but today I had four friend requests—from Dodi, Jake Lyall, Tom Myers, and Colin Morgan.

"What do I do?" I asked Flora, who was looking over my shoulder.

She rolled her eyes. "You just click on Accept."

"But I'm not sure I want to be friends with any of them."

"No wonder you're so lonely," said Flora.

I wasn't going to click yes for Dodi, but Flora made me. "Beggars can't be choosers," she said, and I guess she's right.

THURSDAY, NOVEMBER 3

Grandma's plans all fell through today. The waves were too small for surfing and the ground was too wet for riding, and the Babes flatly refused to go for a walk. Then Dad called to announce he was coming down for a surprise visit because he had a meeting in Exeter, and Grandma bundled the Babes into the car to go shopping.

"Sure you won't come with us?" she asked, but Flora announced she had to do her roots and I shook my head because suddenly, more than anything in the world, I wanted to be alone.

Grandma and the Babes drove off. Flora went inside, and I started to walk, very slowly, toward our tree.

I don't even know what sort of tree it is, just that it was

always hers and mine and that it's old and good for climbing, with a sort of platform halfway up which is hidden even in winter, when the leaves are fallen. It's been a lot of things, that tree. It's been Tintagel and Camelot, a Roman chariot and a pirate ship, and it was *ours*. It's the one place I know that I can always find her, and when I climbed up she was waiting. She is always waiting.

I reached the platform and I closed my eyes and laid my cheek against the trunk. I swear, I could *see* her. I spread my hand out on the wood and it was like the tree had become her. I curled up with my arms around her and I cried and cried and cried until I heard the car come back and Grandma call me, and then I ran to the stream and held my head underwater until I thought it was going to burst.

Grandma didn't say anything when she saw me dripping wet. This afternoon she sent me out to muck out and brush the ponies and this evening, when all the others were so excited to see Dad, she made me help her with dinner. Grandma may not be a very kissy grandmother, but when we had finished she said, *"Well done, Bluebell,"* very quietly, and I knew that she wasn't just talking about my Yorkshire puddings.

Flora checked her e-mails again after dinner. Grandma says now that Pandora's box has been opened she is resigned to it never being closed again, but she is trying to ration us to fifteen minutes each in the evening, as long as we have done something outdoors during the day. Flora tapped away furiously for way more than fifteen minutes. I wasn't even going to look, but when she said *your turn* I didn't know how to say no. And I'm glad about that because I had an e-mail from Joss.

Joss said that things were very, very quiet in London. His parents and grandparents un-grounded him for the first weekend of half term and he went back to Guildford to see his old friends, but now he is back in Chatsworth Square being made to do endless chores and schoolwork. He said how weird it was without all the shouting and thumping and slamming doors from our house. Zoran goes out to feed the rats every morning, but other than that, and the occasional burst of opera, there's no sign of life at all. *Write to me before I die of boredom!* he said. *What are you all doing? What color is Flora's hair today? I need a Bluebird fix to stop me from going nuts!*

He came online while I was reading, and that's when Grandma's fifteen-minute rule went out the window. He wanted to know everything, so I told him all about the horses and the rain and Flora and me galloping and falling off, and I told him about filming the others gardening and he said he'd love to see that, especially Jas dressed as a Russian peasant and Flora on her knees in the mud. And then we just chatted about nothing, and everything, like I told him about the Facebook friend requests and he said he would send me one, too, and I said that Flora can cook now and is going to make us peanut butter cookies, and he said he wished he could be with us to taste them and I said I wished he was here, too.

And then I told him about today. I said, "There is something I have to tell you," and he said, "That sounds ominous," and then I just came out with it. I said, "I used to have a twin sister but she died three years ago this Christmas." Just like that. One sentence. It felt so easy but afterward I wanted to laugh and cry all at once, because I have never told anyone about it before; I have never said those words. Joss swore and asked why I hadn't told him earlier, and I said because it didn't feel right, and then I told him about the tree and crying with my arms around Iris and that this was the first time since she died that I have told anyone about it. Joss said that he was deeply honored, and I cried a bit more, and then we said good night and logged off at the same time.

I'm still in the study now. I am sitting on the window seat, behind the padded tartan curtain. It is completely dark outside, like it never gets in London. I can just make out the trees in the garden, blowing this way and that in the wind. I'm so tired, but I don't want to go to bed.

THE FILM DIARIES OF BLUEBELL GADSBY
SCENE NINE (TRANSCRIPT)
HAPPY FAMILIES

EXTERIOR. SUNSHINE!!!

JASMINE and TWIG are fighting a duel in the walled
garden at Horsehill Farm. They use long sticks which
they hold with both hands. Twig is merciless in attack,
but Jasmine is nimble in defense, which means she
runs away whenever he comes in for a strike. FLORA
lies on the low branch of a magnolia tree, apparently
asleep. FATHER sits in a deck chair, supposedly watching but secretly writing in a notebook.

> TWIG
> (roars)
> STAND STILL AND FIGHT LIKE A KNIGHT!!!

> JASMINE
> (shrieks and hides behind Father's deck chair)
> Save me, Daddy, save me!

FATHER

(absentminded, not looking up)

Fair maiden, thou must learn to defend thyself.

Flora frowns, opens her eyes, and peels herself off the tree, calls Twig and Jas over, takes their sticks, and creeps up to Father's deck chair.

FLORA

(poking deck chair really quite hard)

ON GUARD, YOU COWARD!!!

Father is good, but Flora is better, the result of endless fencing lessons as a child. She dances around him, laughs as she parries his blows, shouts "ha!" when he stumbles under her attack. She disarms him with an elegant flick of the wrist and forces him to kneel before her in the wet grass. She places one foot on his shoulder and raises her stick to the sky. In her purple Wellington boots, with Grandma's duffle coat over her pajamas and her pink and purple dreadlocks tumbling down her back, she looks mad but also strangely warrior-like.

FLORA

Ignoble knight! Do you yield?

FATHER
Never!

FLORA
(pokes him with her stick)
DO YOU YIELD?

FATHER
I yield!

FLORA
KNIGHTS! TO ARMS!!

Jasmine and Twig launch themselves at Father.
GRANDMA storms out of the house. For all her child
slavery/cold water swimming/galloping on horseback
philosophy, she has a rule about rolling around in wet
grass, which is that you shouldn't do it. She is about to
shout, but her face softens at the sight of Dad crying
with laughter, being tickled by Jasmine and Twig. She
smiles. Even Flora is laughing. The camera turns away
from them and up, to where puffy white clouds chase
each other across the blue, blue sky.

It is hard to believe anything bad could happen in a
place like this.

Last night when I went to bed, Flora was waiting for me, looking troubled because she had just eavesdropped on a conversation between Dad and Grandma in the kitchen. Basically, Grandma was angry with Dad because he says he has to leave tomorrow, and with Mum because she is not here at all.

"What can I tell you?" said Dad. "She's needed in Beijing."

"SHE'S NEEDED HERE!" shouted Grandma. "THESE CHILDREN NEED THEIR PARENTS!"

Dad said we were fine, which Flora says is just typical. Flora says, of course we *are* fine, but Dad would say that even if we were in the middle of an earthquake, and a towering inferno to go with it. And then Dad said, very quietly but loud enough for Flora to hear, "Do you remember what Papa said when you left London to come and live here? He said, you had both always dreamed of living in the country, and now you were following your dream. I'm happy, Mum. I'm doing something that makes me happy, and for the first time in three years I don't wake up every morning wanting to scream." Grandma said, "But what about your family?" and Dad said he would tell us soon enough and when he did he was sure we would understand. And then Grandma asked what Mum thought of

115

all this, and Dad sounded really sad and said he couldn't remember the last time he and Mum had a conversation without arguing.

Now, Flora is more convinced than ever that Dad is in love with someone in Warwick. Some weird teacher type from the uni. She said they probably read their books out loud to each other in bed, and that she was very pessimistic about the future. But then in the end, Dad did stay. He was all set to go back after the tickling frenzy on the lawn but then Jas clung to his legs, and Twig explained (very slowly, like Dad was the child and Twig was the grown-up) that we had built a bonfire and that for supper there would be sausages and baked potatoes and marshmallows, and also fireworks in the village.

"You *have* to stay, Daddy," said Jas, and then she did her round cat's eyes and Dad sighed and said what the hell, all right, he would stay and we could all go home together on the train.

So Dad came bodysurfing with us, and even though he yelled when he went in the water (he got a wet suit without socks, which is not a mistake he will ever repeat), afterward he couldn't stop talking about it.

"Remember when we all caught that same wave?" he said.

Also, "I haven't had that much fun in ages!"

And, "Why don't I do this every year?" forgetting that

whenever Grandma makes us do this on New Year's Day, he stays at home by the fire and sleeps.

When we were warm and dry again, we built the bonfire. We piled up all the wood we had gathered over the week, along with all the junk Grandma had hoarded for a year: newspapers, vegetable crates, cardboard boxes, a broken chair, rotten floorboards from the old shed, piling it as high as we could. We drove to the village for the fireworks display, and then came home to light the fire, and Dad made us hold hands and dance around it. We ate the sausages and potatoes, and then Grandma brought out blankets and we wrapped them around ourselves and lay on our backs to watch the stars, all except Flora who toasted marshmallows for us while Dad told ghost stories.

"Mummy would love this," said Jas, when the stories were finished and we were all quiet watching the flames.

"She would." Dad held out his arms and Jas climbed onto his lap. He held her close and buried his face in her hair, rocking her.

"I wish she was here," Jas said, and Dad said, "So do I, sausage," and carried on rocking.

My eyes met Flora's across the bonfire, and she shrugged.

We are on the train now. It was sad to say good-bye to Grandma, but I'm looking forward to seeing Joss. At least,

I think I am. How do you behave with people when you have told them your innermost secret? Not that Iris dying is a secret, exactly, but that's how it felt to me. Will he want to talk about it? Will he want to know what happened? Maybe he will just behave exactly as he always has, and if he does, will I be relieved or disappointed? Maybe, he won't say anything immediately but will wait for an opportune moment, and then maybe when that happens I will start to talk and talk like I always do with him, and maybe it will feel good.

Maybe.

LONDON

I have been thinking about Iris and how she used to climb our tree, up and up, fearless, until she reached the top when I was always too scared to go higher than the platform. I once told Grandma it wasn't fair that Iris was so much braver than me. Iris was never afraid of anything, but Grandma said that there's a difference between being brave and not being afraid. Iris was not afraid because Iris never thought about the consequences of what she did. "Iris is a doer," Grandma said. "You, Blue, actually think about what could happen to you if you fell out of that tree. The day you do climb to the top, you will be much braver than she is." So I gritted my teeth and I did it. Iris shot up before me, and I just climbed on up after her and tried not to look down, until I was next to her and we were both screaming our heads off because we were on top of the world together.

I am not the joyous, triumphant person who once climbed right to the top of that tree.

I am not on top of the world.

Joss came around this morning before school. He was wearing this battered green parka over a navy hoodie I have never seen before, and his hair was still wet from the shower. He looked so . . . Joss-like. He gave this great big smile when he saw me, and he put his arm around my shoulders and hugged me and said *How's my Bluebird, I've missed you!*

It was a nice hug and I did feel relieved. I thought, this is going to be all right, everything is still normal, and I was happy. Then before I could think of anything to say, Flora came striding out, in her tartan miniskirt and knee-high Doc Martens, with her multicolored hair piled up on her head. She glared at Joss and he let go of my shoulders and we all marched off to school, keeping up with Flora who walked in between us and went on and on about how excited she was that rehearsals for the Extravaganza were starting again tonight. I rolled my eyes at Joss and he grinned and said, very politely, "You're so lucky. I'd love to be involved in something like that," and Flora asked, "Do you act," and he said, "No, more of a stagehand, me," and then Flora—Flora!—said, "Well, we're always short of stagehands so why don't you come along to rehearsal with me this evening," *and Joss actually said okay.*

I should have known then that something was wrong. I only saw him once at school, at lunch. I felt sick and didn't think I would be able to eat anything but Jake and Tom and Colin, who seem to have decided to adopt me, all dragged me along to the canteen; and there he was ahead of me in line, carrying a lunch tray, on his own as usual but not seeming to mind.

"Afternoon, gorgeous," he said when we met at the cutlery station.

Jake said *join us* (except he sort of squeaked it because

ever since the Great Rat Debacle, he has positively worshipped Joss). Joss laughed and said thank you, but he could see I was in good hands and he didn't want to get in the way of my many admirers, and then he patted me on the shoulder and I blushed. "Catch you later, Bluebird," he said, and the whole canteen looked at me, like "the lush new boy and the invisible silent girl" and even though it was mortifying it was also quite cool.

I waited for him outside school, but he didn't come. I waited for ages, and then I even pretended I had forgotten my French book in the library so I could go back in to look around. School was empty except for Old Dave the caretaker, who has hardly any teeth and got cross with me because he wanted to lock up and I was taking too long. I walked home on my own. When I got there, Flora was already running out of the house, cramming a sandwich into her mouth. I heard Zoran shout, "Take your coat," and she yelled back, "I can't, I'm late," and ran past me down the path to Joss's to bang on the door. He came out almost immediately. "Late," Flora repeated, and then the two of them ran off down the street, turned a corner, and disappeared.

And that is when I knew I do have a crush on Joss.

THE FILM DIARIES OF BLUEBELL GADSBY
SCENE TEN (TRANSCRIPT)
BETRAYAL

NIGHT, CHATSWORTH SQUARE.

The darkness is punctuated by pools of orange street-light, the stark silhouettes of winter trees.

A woman walks toward the camera, a work bag slung over her shoulder, a plastic grocery bag hanging from her hand.

A cyclist unlocks his bike from a railing, slides on his lights, and rides down the street toward Ladbroke Grove.

A gray fox trots along the pavement, brush thin and ragged, nose held high. He slips through the railings into a garden and the camera picks up the faint clatter of a dustbin lid falling. He reappears moments later, licking his chops.

No movement now. Even the wind has stopped.

A couple comes around the corner from Mandeville Crescent, a girl and a boy, walking close together. She wears a green parka which is much too big for her. He wears a navy hoodie and is hugging himself against the cold.

They are FLORA and JOSS.

They stop outside the gate. They do not look at the house, do not notice the open window, the camera looking down at them. Their words are only just audible.

> FLORA
> Thank you for lending me your coat.

> JOSS
> Anytime.
> (pause)

> JOSS (cont.)
> It looks good on you.
> (Pause. Flora looks away.)

> JOSS (cont.)
> But then everything looks good on you.

FLORA

I should go in.

JOSS

(reaching out to touch Flora's hair)

Flora.

He steps toward her and now Flora is not looking
away. She looks straight at him as he moves closer, as
he bends down, as he slips his hand from her hair to
her neck, drawing her closer to him.

He kisses her.

She kisses him back.

The camera goes black.

TUESDAY, NOVEMBER 8

This morning we received a postcard from Dad:

If King Arthur had a daughter, what would she be like?

I think it says a lot about my family that nobody actually
stopped to say, *I wonder why Dad is asking that*, or, *I'm well,
too, Dad thanks for asking*. They just launched straight in.

"She would be drippy," said Twig. "She would hang out of her chamber window in her tower bleating *save me, Daddy, save me.*"

Jas scowled and kicked him, but Twig jumped out of the way, laughing. "She would be brave," growled Jas. "She would slay dragons and rescue ladies and KILL STUPID USELESS KNIGHTS!!"

"Then she wouldn't be a daughter, she'd be a son," said Twig.

Jas threw her homework book at him.

"What do you think, Flora?" asked Zoran.

"About what?"

Flora has been wandering around in a little bubbly cloud of happiness. It is almost impossible to get her attention, let alone have a conversation with her.

"If King Arthur had a daughter," said Zoran, "what would she be like?"

Flora sighed, like she was saying we were all too silly, but she was so full of goodwill and sweetness and light she was going to answer us anyway. "She'd have awesome clothes," she said. "Suits of armor to fight in, and flowing robes."

"Flowing robes!" scoffed Twig. "Dad's gone nuts."

"Your father is a great intellectual," said Zoran.

"Is he?" asked Jas. "Really, truly great?"

Flora snorted. Zoran glared. Jas burst into tears and said she wished we were still in Devon.

I was the only one who didn't say anything, but then I was also the only one who bothered to reply to Dad.

If King Arthur had a daughter, I e-mailed him this evening, *she would be very confused.*

I almost didn't go to school today. Zoran had to come into my room and practically drag me out of bed. I told him I didn't feel well but he wouldn't listen. He said, "I have a lot of things to do today which do not involve me staying at home looking after little girls who are actually quite well enough to go to school." I told him I could stay on my own and he said no, that Mum and Dad pay him to look after me and so I have to go.

"If I die," I said, "my blood will be on your hands."

"Leave the dramatics to Flora," said Zoran. "They don't suit you."

"I HATE YOU!" I screamed as he walked off down the stairs. "AND I AM NOT A LITTLE GIRL!"

"You certainly sound like one." Flora emerged from her bedroom and yawned. She was wearing her green and pink silk kimono, the one she used to say makes her look too girly. Her hair hung down her back like a tangled, dreadlocked rainbow. She looked weird and glamorous and beautiful, and the sight of her made me scream again.

Afterward I regretted it, of course. I scuttled off to school without waiting for her because I couldn't bear to be there while she told Joss how childish I had been. "Blue threw a tantrum this morning!" I could just imagine her saying. "She screamed her head off like a two-year-old." And Joss would answer, "I thought I heard something through the walls; wow, Bluebird, I never knew you had it in you," and then he and Flora would probably kiss again, in public, in the street, in front of me, and I would have to be all "oh, you two are so cute together," or make puking noises, or pretend not to notice or whatever it is you are supposed to say or do when you are twelve years old and your big sister is KISSING THE BOY YOU LOVE RIGHT IN FRONT OF YOU.

The boy I love?

At school I did my best to ignore everyone. You would think after all these months of being ignored myself it would be easy, but apparently this is not possible when you have caused a sensation by bringing race car–driving rats into school. For a start, Dodi brought me cupcakes. "I made them last night and remembered you used to like them," she said.

CUPCAKES? I BECOME HER FRIEND ON FACE-BOOK AND SHE BRINGS ME CUPCAKES? AFTER YEARS OF IGNORING ME? AFTER I PUBLICLY HUMILIATED HER?

Still, they were the Red Velvet ones with cream cheese icing that Jas loves, so I took them for her, except then Dodi looked disappointed so I ended up sharing them with her at break, even though we didn't exactly speak to each other while we ate them. And in French, waiting for La Gilbert, Jake Lyall rocked up with his two musketeers, and I flipped when they all tried to show me drawings of skateboarding rats they want to use to decorate their boards.

"OH WHAT'S THE POINT?" I shouted. They looked shocked. Basically nobody is used to me shouting, ever.

"Your rats are famous," said Jake.

"They're really cool," stammered Colin.

"THEY'RE, LIKE, MEGASTARS," shouted Tom, even more loudly than me, but then Tom is like Grandma and always shouts so no one batted an eye.

"I meant what's the point of living," I said. I slumped over my desk and tried to ignore them, but I think boys are programmed not to get the "I want to be alone" thing because they just hung around until I looked at their drawings, which are admittedly quite cool.

I went out again at lunchtime. I slipped out through the gate like my old invisible self and went back to Home Sweet Home. It was just like it always has been: the old smelly dog and Capital Radio, the men in black-framed glasses waving their iPads, the mums with their strollers. I remembered sitting here with Joss, the way he decided what I needed to feel better, the cakes he ordered, the way he listened when I told him stuff I've never told anyone, and I could have screamed again.

There was a baby at the table next to me, all wrapped in white except for a pink ribbon in her corkscrew curls, her skin smooth and shiny and black, fast asleep with her hands scrunched up by her face like babies do, like they're saying *please don't wake me, please, however cute you think I am, please don't coo and poke me and wake me up.* And I wished I could be like her.

The baby woke up anyway and looked straight at me. Her eyes were like chocolate. She reached out her hand and I held mine out without thinking so that she could grab my finger. She gurgled. Her mother smiled.

"She likes you," she said.

"I like her," I replied.

"Shouldn't you be at school?" she asked.

"I'm going back," I sighed.

She had a lovely smile, that woman. "Can't be that bad, sweetheart," she said

"Believe me, it is," I said.

Nobody saw me slip back into school. Even today, when my blood boils with anger, when if I let myself I could shout loud enough to bring every teacher, every classroom assistant, every pupil and lunch lady and handyman out from behind all those closed doors and windows, even to-day I can make myself fade to a shadow.

THE FILM DIARIES OF BLUEBELL GADSBY
SCENE ELEVEN (TRANSCRIPT)
A VERY UNLIKELY DAY OUT BUT A PLEASANT BREAK FROM THE TRAGEDY THAT IS MY LIFE

DAYTIME, INSIDE THE RICHMOND HILL RETIRE-
MENT HOME

A large room, shabby but pleasant. Worn beige carpet,
French doors onto a garden. A big table covered in
magazines. Bookcases full of books. Lots and lots of
armchairs covered in flowery fabric, all turned toward
the back of the room where ZORAN sits at an upright
piano. There is a very, very old person in each of the
armchairs. Some of these old people are asleep, a few
dribble but most are alert, their faces bright with expec-
tation. The OLD LADY closest to the piano clasps her
hands to her bosom. She wears her snowy hair pinned
up and gazes adoringly at Zoran. AN OLD MAN IN A
RED BOW TIE beside her gazes adoringly at *her*, but
she pays no attention to him. Zoran sits with his hands
splayed across the keyboard. The old people watch him.

ZORAN

(looks up from the piano)

Chopin, *Nocturne.*

Zoran begins to play, except that play does not seem
the right word. Music pours from the ends of his
fingers, light, haunting, a little sad. The old people
who were asleep wake up. Some of the ones who were
awake close their eyes. The old lady with snowy hair
reaches out for the hand of the old man with the red
bow tie, who goes bright red but beams from ear to
ear. Zoran plays on.

ZORAN

Mazurka!

Zoran's hands dance, drum, fly. People smile. An old
man taps his feet. Two old ladies sway. The old lady
with the snowy hair laughs under her breath. The music finishes. Everyone is awake now.

OLD MAN IN RED BOW TIE

(looking shyly at Old Lady)

Play us a song now, son!

OLD MAN IN GRAY SWEATPANTS

Play something by the Beatles!

Zoran plays "A Hard Day's Night," "All You Need
Is Love," and "Hey Jude." Then he plays "Stormy
Weather," "Puttin' on the Ritz," and "Strangers in the
Night." He plays songs by Buddy Holly and Elvis Pres-
ley. He sings along to all of them. Lots of old people
join in, most with quavering voices, some surprisingly
true. Zoran is transformed. *Au revoir* quiet, geeky au
pair. *Bonjour*, dashing young musician. His curly hair is
a mess from being pushed back between numbers. He
takes his glasses off and his eyes shine. He laughs and
smiles. He exudes confidence and happiness.

The snowy haired old lady and the old man in the bow
tie gaze at each other. When Zoran finishes, half the old
people are in tears, but they are all applauding wildly.

WEDNESDAY, NOVEMBER 9

"I can't go to school," I told Zoran again this morning. "I
just can't."

Zoran put his hand on my forehead, which is what he
always does when we don't feel well, is very unscientific

and always leads to the same result, even when Jas was really sick with an ear infection.

"You're still not ill," he said.

"I have an enormous pain *here*," I said, pointing to my stomach, my heart, and my throat. "Also here," I added, rubbing my head, which was true. It came on just as I was thinking about it.

"What you mean," said Zoran, "is that you don't *want* to go to school."

"Please, Zoran?" I begged. Because I wasn't lying. I *can't* go to school. I can't watch Flora and Joss together. I can't speak to him. I just can't.

I don't know why Zoran didn't tell us about his great-aunt before. She is the snowy haired lady who kept holding the old man's hand. Her name is Alina, and Zoran lived with her all the time he was growing up because his parents were dead.

"She isn't English?" I said.

"She is from Bosnia," said Zoran. "Like me," he added. "But she came here a long time before the war."

I said, "What war," and also that I was surprised because when he speaks he sounds just like us. I didn't even realize he was foreign.

"There was a terrible war in my country," he said. "From

April 1992 to November 1995. Really, I don't know what they teach you at that school. No wonder you don't want to go. And Blue, my name is *Zoran*."

I shrugged. "Lots of people have strange names."

Zoran said in Bosnia his name was not considered strange, and that he didn't want to talk about it anymore.

Alina is lovely. After the concert, she gave me a boiled sweet out of the tin Zoran brought her and told me I was beautiful. Which was comforting, even if she is obviously half blind.

"Is the old man her boyfriend?" I asked.

"Peter? He would like to be. He actually keeps proposing but she always says no."

"That's so sad."

"For heaven's sake, Blue, she is ninety-five years old!"

"I don't see why that matters, if they love each other."

Zoran said, *"I suspect he's only after her money."* I got upset and said I didn't think that was true because the old man looked really sweet and maybe sometimes people really do love each other and Zoran said I was probably right and not to pay attention to him because he was just bitter and twisted.

"I can't believe you never told us about her," I said. "Your great-aunt, I mean."

Zoran said, he wanted to keep his work life and his private life separate.

"I didn't realize we were *work*," I grumbled.

"Childhood and adulthood, if you prefer," he said. "Then and now. Bosnia and England."

"But you grew up *here*," I said.

"That's not the point," said Zoran. "And you should have piano lessons. I can't believe none of you play a musical instrument."

"Flora did start learning the violin," I said. "But she got bored. We were all quite relieved, to be honest."

"Music is a great healer," said Zoran. Suddenly he looked really sad.

"You looked different when you were playing," I told him. "Almost handsome."

Zoran laughed. *"Almost?"* he said, and I laughed, too.

Zoran goes to the old people's home once during the week when we are at school, and also over the weekend when Mum and Dad are here. Every time he goes, they ask him to play the piano.

"Don't you mind?" I asked.

He doesn't mind, because that is the only time he gets to play. His great-aunt sold her baby grand at the same time as her house in order to pay for the Richmond Hill Retirement Home, so now he has no home of his own, and no instrument.

"You must miss it," I said, meaning the home.

"Every day," he replied, meaning the piano.

. . .

I felt a teeny bit better about life when we got back. We had lunch and Zoran told me about his thesis which is called something like LIGHT IN THE DARKNESS: MAGIC AND METAPHYSICS IN TWELFTH-CENTURY BRITAIN. I actually have no idea what it's about, but he got very excited about it. He started it three years ago when he was twenty-two, and he says he hopes to finish next year, if we ever give him a bit of peace. After lunch he put on a CD of a Russian composer called Rachmaninoff and sat in the study to work, and I lay on my bed to write up this diary. Then at three thirty we went to pick the Babes up from school. We took them to the park, and we went to the café and had those sticky baked custard pies and hot chocolate with whipped cream on top. We all got cream on our nose, and Zoran took a picture of us on his phone, which he kept as his screensaver. It was so cozy and the whole day was so different I actually almost forgot about all the horribleness and sadness and disappointment of yesterday.

Then we went home, and Flora was there with Joss. Kissing in the kitchen.

It turns out I am not as invisible as I thought I was. I went back to Home Sweet Home for lunch, and the cute baby was there again. Her mother, who is called Ash, told me the baby's name is Pretty.

"Because she is," said Ash. "Would you like to give her her bottle?"

Ash told me all about what it was like to have a little baby, how neither she nor Pretty sleep at night but they nap all morning, tucked up together in Ash's big bed when her boyfriend goes to work. She bought me rhubarb crumble and insisted I have custard with it, and made a big fuss about me getting back to school on time. I felt almost happy when I left—kind of stupefied by the amount of pudding I'd eaten, and warm and fuzzy from holding Pretty and being fussed over by Ash, but then it was ruined by Madame Gilbert at the gate, who was still on her mobile but now has it in for me, so is not laid-back any more *at all.*

She called me rat girl—or more precisely *hey, you, rat girl!*—and put me in detention. Which in itself wasn't a problem, because it meant I could avoid the whole potential walking home from school with the happy couple, but when I did get home they were blocking the front path, with Flora and Zoran yelling at each other.

"It's not my fault the rehearsal schedule's been acceler-
ated!" Flora was shouting. "This isn't some school play, you
know. This is professional theater!"

"An amateur dramatics pantomime is not professional
theater," said Zoran. "Nor is it a university degree."

"So WHAT?" cried Flora.

"So do your homework and then you can go."

"YOU'RE NOT MY MOTHER!!!" screamed Flora.

"Come on, dude," said Joss. "Be cool."

He smiled at me, like he was saying, "Tell him, Blue." I
shrugged. He raised his eyebrows. I looked away.

"*You* do *not* call me *dude*," said Zoran, not shouting but
sounding so cold I actually shivered. I must have made a
noise, because he turned around to look at me and even in
the dark, with Joss standing just behind him and my heart
thudding so hard I thought I was going to be sick, I could
see that he was furious.

"Ah," said Zoran. "The wanderer returns."

Flora started backing down the path. She has always
been good at spotting opportunities.

"I'll be back by nine," she called out when she reached
the gate.

"I HAVEN'T FINISHED WITH YOU!!" roared Zoran,
but she was already running down the street, hand in hand
with Joss.

"I promise I'll do my homework when I get back!" she

shouted, except she was laughing so much you could barely make out the words.

She wasn't home by nine. I went up to bed and lay there listening for her, and listening to the sound of Zoran pacing up and down the hallway, waiting. There was more shouting when she came in, and tears. I put my pillow over my head and tried to block it out.

FRIDAY, NOVEMBER 11

Mum came home today. We were expecting her for supper, but her plane was delayed. Zoran looked up the details on the web, and Jas cried when he said she wouldn't land till eleven fifteen. Twig didn't cry but went down to the garden to talk to the rats. Flora slammed out of the house to see Joss, then slammed back in again because he was out. Zoran shouted at her.

I stayed in my room with my camera, replaying The Kiss.

So far I have managed to avoid Joss quite well, but presumably one day I will have to speak to him again. He is my neighbor, after all, as well as my sister's boyfriend. Who knows, maybe one day he will even be my brother-in-law.

The way she slips out of his coat. The way she looks at him, half laughing. Straight at him, *inviting* him to kiss her. I tried to tell myself she didn't give him a choice, but then . . .

The way he touches her hair, slips his hand behind her neck . . .

Kiss.

Pause.

Rewind.

The way she slips out of his coat . . .

The way he touches her hair . . .

It's so obvious he wanted her, too.

We didn't eat together this evening. Flora took her plate up to her room and Twig took his back out into the garden. Zoran, Jas, and I ate in front of the TV—salmon *en croute* with homemade mayonnaise, potato wedges, and lemon tart.

"You've surpassed yourself," I told Zoran, because it was true and also because he looked miserable. He shrugged and said he knew it was quite common for teenagers to eat in their bedrooms but did we think it entirely normal for Twig to eat in the garden, in the dark, with the rats, when it was beginning to rain, and also did we think it means he is a failure as an au pair?

Then Twig came in and had to have a very hot bath because he was soaked through and freezing, but instead of shampoo he accidentally used the new Chanel bath milk sample Mum gave Jas last time she was home, and Jas went ballistic. It has been a while since she threw a proper tantrum, as opposed to just crying, and I had forgotten just how loud she can shout and how extreme she can be. She shouted that she hates us all, especially Twig, and she hopes we all die soon so she can have some peace and quiet in her life free from thieves like her horrible brother, and she wishes she had never been born. When Zoran tried to calm her down, she bit him. Then she threw Twig's entire comic book collection down the stairs, went to bed, and cried herself to sleep. Twig crept out of the bathroom smelling delicious but looking rather scared and asked if he could sleep with me tonight. Flora stayed in her room.

I sat up in bed with the lights off for Twig's sake, typing up my diary and listening to him asleep on the mattress beside my bed. He does these little snorts and grunts which make him sound like a piglet. All the way downstairs, Zoran was listening to a concert on the radio in the kitchen, and occasional bursts of music or applause drifted up so I could hear.

It's been a long time since I had the dream of the beach in Devon where Dad once made us scream. It's always the same: low tide, with shelves of pebbles leading down toward the water edge where the shingle is sand colored and gleaming in the shallow surf and the occasional piece of sea glass glints like treasure. Except for the orangey shingle and the dull green of fields high above us on the cliff tops, the landscape is practically monochrome. Cliffs, sea, sky, everything is gray. A white mist is creeping in from the sea and through that mist a figure appears, thin and frail, walking away from where I stand with Mum and Dad, Flora, Jas, and Twig. The mist shifts in the wind. The figure grows dim, then solid, then dim again. Every time she reappears, she is a little smaller, until she vanishes completely.

She doesn't look back.

I knew Mum was home as soon as I woke up. There were real voices downstairs, and the house just felt less empty. I don't think I have ever in my entire life felt so happy at the thought of seeing her. I slipped out of bed and out of my room, across the landing and down the stairs, quietly so as not to wake the others. Tonight I didn't want to share her, or wait my turn until the others shut up. I wanted Mum, *now*. Her arms holding me, her voice telling me she loved me. I can't describe how much I wanted it. It was like a *hunger*.

I stopped when I reached the kitchen door. Something was wrong. Mum wasn't getting to her feet to welcome me. She sat with her back to the door with her head in her hands. Zoran sat beside her. "I don't like it any more than they do," she was saying.

"But do you *have* to travel so much?" asked Zoran.

"In this job, yes. I've asked to do less, of course, but they have made it quite clear it wasn't an option."

"So quit," said Zoran.

"Quit?" Mum sounded appalled.

"I'm not sure I can cope anymore," Zoran said. "Jas doesn't stop crying, I'm worried about Blue, and Flora has become uncontrollable."

"Work," said Mum in a strange low voice, "is the only place where I don't think about my daughter."

And then she began to cry, rocking back and forth on her chair, her arms wrapped around her middle. "Iris, my baby, my baby!"

Zoran shifted around so that he was facing her and took her hands. She leaned her head on his shoulder and sobbed.

"I know," said Zoran. "Believe me, Cassie, I know."

I heard a noise behind me. Flora was sitting on the stairs, looking like she'd been turned to stone.

"It wasn't my fault," I whispered.

Flora didn't answer. We crept back up the stairs and into bed and we didn't speak another word.

SATURDAY, NOVEMBER 12

> **Fault** *n* **1** a failing or defect; flaw. **2** a mistake or error. **3** a misdeed. **4** responsibility for a mistake or misdeed.

Of the three of us, Iris was always the one coming up with ideas, and so she was our leader. Dodi and I were her not-quite partners in crime, her faithful lieutenants, and also her babysitters, because a person who isn't afraid of anything is also a person who needs looking after. The long pretend games. The pet grooming salon in Year five. The trying to sail around the entire lake on a sailing course when we were meant to stay between the buoys. We did them all, but we stopped short of eating the plants she insisted were real food in our pretend games. We shampooed the neighborhood cats, but drew the line at using a hair dryer. We called for help when she said we should paddle.

We looked after her. We were *always* looking after her.

Yesterday was Armistice Day. We did the two-minute silence thing at eleven o'clock, to mark the end of World War I on the eleventh hour of the eleventh day of the eleventh month. We had to stay behind at the end of math and stand in front of our desks, with Mr. Math glaring at us. Anthea told us in English that his brother is a soldier and was injured in Afghanistan and no one dared move a muscle for the whole two minutes. But at the end, when they blew the bugle and said, "We will remember them," I saw Dodi wipe her eyes and I know it wasn't for Mr. Math's brother.

THE FILM DIARIES OF BLUEBELL GADSBY
SCENE TWELVE
JOSS AND FLORA

NIGHTTIME. THE GARDEN, AGAIN, VIEWED FROM
THE ROOF OUTSIDE CAMERAMAN (BLUE)'S BED-
ROOM WINDOW. CLOUDY NIGHT. LEAFLESS TREES.
THE OCCASIONAL SWOOP OF A BAT.

Camera slowly scans wall and trellis before resting on
the Batemans' house. More specifically, on the balcony
of Joss's attic bedroom. The angle is difficult and the
camera can only catch a sidelong view, but as the balcony doors open, it picks up the sound of Bob Marley
singing "One Love." FLORA and JOSS appear, silhou-
etted against the light. Joss drapes his arm around
Flora, pulls her close. They kiss. She leans her head
on his shoulder.

SUNDAY, NOVEMBER 13

Today is Twig's birthday. He got his sleeping bag, like he

asked for. Zoran gave him a Swiss Army knife and I got him the SAS Survival Guide. We had cake and candles this afternoon. Last night, Mum, Twig, and Jas went to the Natural History Museum with six boys from Twig's class. They did ask if I wanted to go, but I wasn't in the mood, so I stayed home with Zoran while they ran around with dinosaurs and Flora was next door with Joss while his grandparents went to the theater.

There is nothing else to say.

MONDAY, NOVEMBER 14

I tried to look ill when I came down to breakfast, but the Babes had got there before me and nobody took a blind bit of notice. They were all arguing and looking exhausted because none of them slept at all on Saturday night.

"It's not fair!" Twig was raging. "*Why* do we have to go to school when you are here? *Why?*"

"But I am *not* here!" cried Mum. "I have to go to the office! I have meetings! I won't be at home, so why should you be?"

"We don't expect you to stay at home," whispered Jas. "We know you have to work. We want to come to the office with you."

I sighed and drooped hopefully over my cornflakes.

Nobody noticed except Zoran, who just rolled his eyes.

"I can't possibly take you to the office, darlings," said Mum. "It's just not done."

"Then I don't see the point of you coming home *at all,*" said Jas. "Come on, Twig. Let's go to school."

The Babes marched out of the kitchen with their noses in the air.

"Wait!" Mum tried to drain her coffee cup and spilled it down her blouse. "You can't go alone! Darlings, wait, I have to change my shirt! You musn't go alone!"

"Please don't let us keep you from your fascinating job," Jas called out from the hall.

My eight-year-old sister standing up for herself.

"You're not ill, Blue," said Zoran when they'd all gone. "Whatever music it is, you can't keep avoiding it."

"Life," I said, "is not all about music."

"Nice if it was though," said Zoran, but I was already on my way out, even though it wasn't even eight o'clock yet. I have been leaving early to avoid Joss and Flora, but today when I flung open the door he was already leaning against our garden wall, waiting.

"Flora's not ready," I said.

"Actually," he said, "I was waiting for you."

I couldn't think of anything to say to that. I think I blushed. I may have said "oh." All I know for sure is that we started walking.

Together.

Me and him.

"It's been ages since we last talked," he said.

I managed to squeak something about being busy. Joss said, "I just wanted to make sure, you know, that you're cool with me and Flora," and I sort of laughed and said, "Oh, super cool, I think it's great," and he said that was a relief, because he really valued our friendship and he didn't want me to think that just because he was going out with my big sister we couldn't be friends.

My *big* sister. I tried to make myself look taller. I may have stuck my chest out. I wished I was wearing something more interesting than jeans and navy All Stars.

"Because I'm always here for you, Blue," Joss was saying. "You know that. All that stuff you wrote me about, your sister and everything. I've talked about it loads with Flora . . ."

Joss has been talking about me with Flora?

"And I want you to know that any time you want to talk to me, I mean any time you feel you need to . . ."

"I don't," I mumbled.

"I'm sorry?"

"I don't talk about Iris with *anybody*!" I thought I was going to cry again. "I can't believe you talked to Flora about her!"

"But Blue, it wasn't anything she didn't know!" Joss had

to break into a run to keep up with me. "I didn't realize it would upset you!"

"IT WAS PRIVATE!" I roared.

I couldn't bear to walk with him after that. I ran on ahead, and he didn't follow.

THURSDAY, NOVEMBER 17

Dodi and I are officially reconciled, I think, and it is largely thanks to Jake Lyall, which just goes to show what a strange turn my life has taken, as Grandma might say.

I hadn't spoken to the boys since they showed me their skateboard designs, but they pounced on me at lunchtime when I tried to sneak off to the library as usual instead of going to the canteen.

"You've got to eat," said Jake.

Colin nodded.

"IF YOU DON'T EAT," yelled Tom, "YOU WILL DIE."

"I am NOT HUNGRY," I said firmly. "And I have homework to finish."

By two o'clock, my tummy was rumbling. Jake looked smug and gave me half a Mars bar. Mr. Math confiscated it.

By three thirty I was so hungry I could have cried. Jake made Colin give me his after-school Twix.

"He doesn't really like them anyway," he said.

"It's true," Colin lied, practically drooling.

"JAKE WANTS YOU TO COME TO THE PARK WITH US," boomed Tom.

Jake went bright red. "It's floodlit until five o'clock," he mumbled. "We thought we could teach you some moves."

"Moves?" I said.

"SKATEBOARDS!" yelled Tom.

"Oh, *cool*!" cried Dodi. I swear she just appeared from nowhere. "Can I come?"

The thing with Dodi is, people still don't know what to say to her since the whole peeing on the floor incident, and even though she's really good at looking like she couldn't care less I know her well enough to know that she minds a *lot*. She stood there looking all cute and cool in her blue jacket and silver beanie and her long blond hair, but the way the boys stared she might as well have been an alien. But then Colin kind of blushed and stammered, "Sure, the more the merrier," and it was like a spell had been broken. Dodi beamed and the boys started messing around and suddenly I was being swept along toward the park without having once said that I wanted to go.

I have never thought about skateboards before. Skateboarding is just something boys like Tom and Jake and Colin do, and I have no interest in it. But in the park this afternoon the same thing happened as when I saw Zoran at the piano. They were different. Not so much Tom and Colin, but Jake was like another person. It's quite hard to know what Jake is thinking most of the time, mainly because he is usually asleep, so it was quite a surprise to see him either concentrating like mad or grinning his head off, and it's funny how people look better when they're happy.

The first time I stood on Jake's skateboard, I tried to move forward by sort of wiggling my bottom, screamed, and fell off.

Dodi got cross and told the boys not to laugh. She said they were rubbish teachers, and then she leaped onto Jake's board and glided around like she was some sort of Mediterranean yacht. It was actually very impressive.

"Unreal," said Jake. They all stared at her, and I could tell that just like that Dodi was cool again. She sailed back up to us, jumped off Jake's board, and flipped it up with her back foot.

"Where d'you learn to skate like that?" whispered Colin.

"Around," shrugged Dodi.

"Teach me," I ordered, then I added "please?" because I sounded so bossy.

We looked at each other for a moment like we did outside the art block after the rat incident, except this was different, too, and then Dodi smiled—not the smirky half smile I have grown used to when she looks at me, but this huge grin which showed off her turquoise train tracks and which made her look like the old Dodi.

"All right then," she said.

The boys messed around on Tom's and Colin's boards, and Dodi showed me how to place my feet and find my balance. She showed me how to move by shifting my weight, and how to protect myself when I fell off, which was loads. We stayed until way after dark, and only left when the park police came around in their car and told us the park was closing. I thanked Dodi when we left her at the end of her street, and she grinned again and rubbed her nose like she always does when she is pleased and embarrassed at the same time and asked if I wanted to walk to school with her.

"Like we used to," she said. I swear I could feel Iris watching us. I don't mean from heaven or wherever she is, I mean she was *right there with us*, just hiding in the shadows.

"Not tomorrow," Dodi said. "I've got to go in early for choir practice, but Monday?"

"Say yes," hissed Iris.

"I'd love to," I said, and I meant it. I really meant it.

I could tell Zoran had been worrying about me when I got home. I thought he was going to get cross, but he took one look at me and said *I've made a cherry and almond cake* instead. He sat with me while I ate three slices and drank two glasses of milk. I told him about my skateboarding lesson and he frowned and said shouldn't I have elbow pads and helmets and stuff.

"Honestly, Zoran," I said, "you're such an old woman."

"I'm just doing my job," he grumbled, but he was smiling. "Your cheeks are pink," he said. "And your nose is very red."

"I'm sorry I forgot to text you," I said.

"Not important." He picked up my plate and dropped a kiss on top of my head as he passed.

FRIDAY, NOVEMBER 18

Flora is trying to stop us from going to see her play.

Normally, Flora is the sort of person who, when people are singing her "Happy Birthday," tells them to sing louder. She is the sort of person who jumps up shouting *me, me!* when they ask for volunteers at the circus. At Grandpa's funeral, they say she danced on the kitchen table in nothing but her underwear and a feather boa she found in the dressing-up box because people weren't paying enough attention to her. Granted, she was only three. But still.

Flora is a show-off. And practically begging us not to come and see her in a play is the opposite of showing off. This was the conversation last night:

FLORA

I just don't think it's suitable for children.

JAS

But it's FAIRY TALES!!!

TWIG

Plus we're not children. Or rather, we are, but so
are you.

FLORA

Excuse me but you are half my age. And these
fairy tales are bloody and gory and extremely
disturbing. Loads of people die in them. At the
end the wicked queen has to dance in burning
slippers until she drops quite dead, and there is
the smell of burning flesh.

TWIG

How many people?

JAS

I hate it when people die.

TWIG

More than in *War and Peace*?

ZORAN

Far fewer than in *War and Peace.* I have looked
on the Players' website and they state quite
clearly that the Christmas Extravaganza is family
entertainment. Your sister is merely suffering
from stage fright.

FLORA

I do *not* suffer from stage fright.

JAS

I'M NOT GOING IF PEOPLE DIE!

ZORAN

Twig and I will go with Blue. Jas, nobody is going
to force you to see a show you don't want to see.
We will find you a babysitter.

FLORA

You *are* the babysitter.

And so on. I think the argument would have gone on
forever, if Dad hadn't come home right in the middle of it
and said damn right, we were all going, because this family
always pulls together, isn't that right, team?

Dad looks different. His hair has grown very long, and

it's sort of shaggy and almost completely gray. He's got these new glasses, the black-rimmed ones like the young men in Home Sweet Home, and even though he still wears the same old tweed jacket it doesn't look quite the same, maybe because he is now wearing it with designer jeans and has an iPhone. It is extremely disconcerting.

"You will hate it," Flora assured him. "It's a completely unprofessional production. The music is terrible and the dancing is even worse."

"All the more reason to support you," said Dad.

Then Twig said *are the slippers really on fire and are they really that gory* and Flora said *yes, Little Red Riding Hood cuts out Hansel's and Gretel's hearts and Prince Charming and Snow White roast the Three Little Pigs for their wedding breakfast* and Jas said *do they actually roast real pigs onstage*, which is when Flora started to scream and ran upstairs shouting that we were ruining her life. Then Dad went upstairs as well, but he didn't go and speak to her. Instead he went into his room, and when he came out half an hour later he was wearing a dinner jacket and had slicked his long hair back. He hugged us all good night and said he had to go to a meeting, and he hoped he would be able to explain everything soon.

So much for family always pulling together. I wish I could ask Flora what she thinks of all this.

This is how yesterday ended.

So Dad went out to his mystery meeting and Flora left shortly afterward, saying that she was going to Tamsin's and not to wait up because she would probably spend the night. I'm not sure Zoran believed her but I think he is tired of fighting with her, so he just shrugged and told her to text him to let him know what she decides to do.

Mum is in Prague at the Bütylicious Annual Sales Conference. The Babes, Zoran, and I ordered Chinese takeout and watched *Kung Fu Panda*, Zoran's idea of a themed evening, which worked surprisingly well, considering Jas hates Chinese food, Zoran only likes films in foreign languages, and Twig stuck two chopsticks up his nose. We went to bed at ten thirty. Flora hadn't texted to say what she was doing, and Zoran was pretending not to mind. I lay in bed listening to him pace up and down, then I heard him put the TV on and the next thing I knew someone was shaking me awake.

"There are burglars in the garden," said Jas.

"Ugh," I said.

"They are throwing pebbles at my window." She pulled on my arm. I stopped trying to sleep.

"Why on earth would burglars throw pebbles at your window?" I asked.

"To break in!" cried Jas.

"That makes no sense at all," I said. "And the last time we thought there was a burglar it turned out to be Zoran."

"Come and look."

The flat roof outside my room means that I can't see down onto the veranda, but the window from the Babes' room looks straight down onto it. Jas and I crept through their bedroom to look.

"Don't let them see you!" whispered Jas. "They might shoot you!"

"They won't shoot me," I hissed.

"How do you know?"

"Because they are not burglars, you idiot!" I whispered more loudly. "They are Joss and Flora, behaving very strangely."

We peered out, still hiding. Joss and Flora *were* being very peculiar. They were standing by the garden steps, at the bottom of the drainpipe Joss used to get up to my window. Flora kept trying to climb up it but, even though she has done it loads of times before, as soon as her feet left the ground she slid straight back down again. She gave up in the end and just stood there at the bottom of the drainpipe with her legs crossed like she does when she's laughing so much it makes her want to pee.

"What *is* the matter with her?" asked Jas.

"She's drunk." We both jumped out of our skins. Twig

was standing just behind us, looking at Flora and Joss through his binoculars. I put my hand over Jas's mouth to stop her from screaming.

"But Flora never drinks," she said when I took my hand away.

"She is behaving just like Dad did the last time we went to the Batemans' Christmas party," said Twig. "When he kept topping up the punch with mini vodka bottles."

"Dad did that?"

Twig said Dad won the mini vodka bottles when they did Secret Santa at work, and he had no idea what to do with them until he got to the Batemans' party and decided it was a deserving cause.

"He danced the polka with Mrs. Bateman." I shuddered, remembering.

"And now Flora is dancing with Joss," said Twig.

We looked out of the window again. Flora and Joss had given up on the drainpipe and were waltzing across the lawn.

"Why are they holding their heads like that?" asked Jas.

"They are sharing iPod speakers," said Twig, who was still using his binoculars.

"I still don't like Joss because of what he did to the rats," said Jas. "But they do look lovely."

Joss raised an arm, quite gracefully, and Flora twirled slowly beneath it. She kept twirling as they walked back toward the house, until she looked dizzy and fell into his arms, all tangled up in iPod cords. She put her arms around his neck and whispered something in his ear. He threw back his head, laughed, and saw us all standing there, watching. He waved at us, then pointed at Flora and the window, as if he was saying *what should I do?*

"We have to help them," said Jas.

"Do we?" I said.

"Yes, Blue," said Jas. "We do."

So we hatched this plan to rescue Flora without attracting Zoran's attention, which involved Twig pretending he had a nightmare and luring Zoran into the kitchen to make him some hot milk, while Jas and I dragged Flora around the side of the house to the street, back in through the front door, and up to her room.

And it would have worked, except that Flora was giggling so much she crashed into the cherrywood table on the landing and smashed the Chinese bowl full of dried rose petals. And then Zoran arrived and tripped over her with Twig's hot milk, and then *Dad* came home, also drunk, and thought we were all playing a game which he tried to join in by shouting *I'm it! I'm it!* and counting to fifty to give us time to hide.

Which we did.

In our beds.

Dad went out early this morning. He said he needed to

work. Zoran told him that was all very well but he is due a day off, and he had told Mum who may not have passed the message on to Dad but he was sorry and he really had to get on with some of his own work, in other words his thesis. He said that at the rate he was going he would be lucky to finish it by the time he's thirty. And then Dad said of course, of course, and you musn't change your plans but he couldn't stay either and then he beamed and said it didn't matter because Flora was here and she could look after the little ones.

"Flora?" we all said.

"She's sixteen," said Dad. "In some countries she would already be married."

He left before any of us could protest.

"Unreal," I said.

"You know, Blue, in some countries *you* could be married," said Zoran.

"Fine," I snapped. "I'll look after the Babes. It's not as if I had anything else to do today."

"Tell your sister to call me when she wakes up," said Zoran.

I have no idea when Flora woke up. Zoran told me we weren't to go out farther than the park, so as soon as he left I raided the housekeeping jar, bundled the Babes into their coats, and took them down to the Electric Cinema where they were showing a rerun of the first *Pirates of the*

Caribbean. Jake texted me to say he was bored and what was I doing today. He met us at the cinema, and afterward we went to Home Sweet Home, where we saw Ash and Pretty and Ash's boyfriend, who is covered in tattoos and kept taking Pretty outside to show her off to people he knew walking by in the street (and also to lots of people he didn't know).

We stopped in the park on the way home. Tom and Colin were on the skateboard ramp, and a bunch of older kids I'd never seen before pulled these incredible stunts, turning somersaults in the air and stuff like you see in films. Jake tried but he just sort of fell out of the sky halfway through his turn. I felt sorry for him because I could see he was trying not to cry, but Twig and Jas laughed their heads off and asked him to do it again, which cheered him up a bit. It was getting dark by the time we got home. Dad was asleep. Flora and Zoran were out. I made tea and put some toast on, then sat down with the Babes to watch *Pirates of the Caribbean 2* on DVD, and it felt cozy and peaceful.

I don't think Dad said anything to Flora about last night, but I know Zoran gave her a lecture. They came back while we were watching the film and I overheard them in the kitchen when I went in to get more toast. Flora was saying, *but it was fun*, almost like she was begging, and Zoran said something completely Zoranish about staying true to yourself and not straying off the rightful path, and then they both stared at me like they were making it clear I had no business listening to their conversation, so I left.

MONDAY, NOVEMBER 21

On the way to school today, Dodi told me that she had just seen Joss and Flora kissing under the railway arches.

"Yuk," I said.

Dodi said she thought they looked cute together.

"Dad's got an iPhone," I told her to change the subject. "And long hair, and he has secret meetings in dinner jackets on Friday nights."

I asked her what she thought it meant. I'd forgotten how serious Dodi can be. She thought about it for quite a long time, then she said that last year her father had spent six weeks in a monastery on a Greek island where they don't allow any women except chickens, and that her mother had called it his midlife crisis.

"Not that chickens are actually women," she added. "Just, they need them for the eggs."

I went to the library at lunchtime. I sat in the armchair right at the back, where it's so dark you can hardly see a thing, and I closed my eyes because I felt so tired and tried to do what Grandma once told me to do, which is imagine my life exactly how I would like it to be. I thought, I'll imagine Joss, that he loves me. I haven't done that before, because it felt pointless and also a bit sad, but today my mind had its own ideas. Instead of a happy place with Joss it took me off to Devon, where I was about five years old and hiding on the window seat with Iris, with Twig a fat pudgy baby taking his first toddling steps toward Flora, who was holding out her arms and laughing, and Jas asleep in a basket. It seemed like a bit of a wasted daydream, when I could have dreamed of anything I wanted, but Dad always says you can't control how your mind works. He was at home when I got back, drinking tea and reading the paper.

"Are you having a midlife crisis?" I asked him.

Dad spat out his tea. I mean he really did. All over the kitchen table.

"Well, are you?" I asked.

"No," he said. "At least, I don't think I am."

"Good," I said. I told him about Dodi's dad and the Greek chickens, and he said that didn't appeal to him at all.

"Though I suppose I have been a bit cryptic lately," he added.

"You've been crummy, Dad," I said. "And I miss you."

Zoran came into the kitchen while Dad was hugging me, looking preoccupied, but he smiled back when I smiled at him and mouthed, should he leave me and Dad alone? I shook my head.

"I promise I'll explain soon," Dad was burbling. "Soon,

all will be revealed and hopefully—*hopefully*—you'll start seeing a lot more of your old dad. But what can I do to make up for things in the meantime?"

Behind him, Zoran opened the fridge and sighed. My brain almost exploded with inspiration.

"A present!" cried Dad. "A book? A necklace? A dress?"

"A piano," I said.

"Right," said Dad. "I was not expecting that."

Behind Dad's back, Zoran smiled.

I grinned back. Poor Dad just looked baffled.

TUESDAY, NOVEMBER 22

Sometimes when I think of Joss it makes me cross, but then he does something nice and it's almost worse.

My timing was off this morning and I couldn't avoid leaving with them. Joss was waiting at the gate. He beamed at both of us, then slung his arm around Flora. She nestled into him and gazed into his eyes like she never wanted to stop. He rubbed her nose with his and kissed her on the lips. She giggled and nuzzled his neck. I looked away and tried not to be sick.

Obviously, that wasn't the nice bit. The nice bit came later, after their argument. I was walking ahead of them so I didn't hear it all, but basically it involved Joss accusing Flora of behaving like a prima donna because she doesn't want his friends to come and see the show, presumably because she wants to make a good impression on them and doesn't think she is likely to do that in a play involving the nation's favorite fairy-tale characters eating each other for breakfast.

"It'll be a laugh," Joss said. "We'll see the play then we'll have a few beers and go to a club. Just because you're not . . ."

Flora told him to shut up. Joss started to laugh and said, "Bluebird, you think my friends should come and see your sister's show, don't you?" and I said, "Of course I do," and he said, "There, you see? Blue agrees with me," and then he put his arm around me.

It lasted all of three seconds and I KNOW I'm pathetic, but still.

It was almost a hug.

"Promise you'll tell them not to come," said Flora.

Joss laughed and pulled her into his arms. It was just like in a film, where the actress says *no, I hate you* and the leading man says *but I love you so much* and the actress goes *oh all right then*. Nauseating, but Joss winked at me as he was kissing Flora, and I couldn't help grinning back at him because he looked so wicked.

"Do those two ever stop?" Dodi joined us at the traffic light and stared at Flora and Joss wrapped around each other, pressed up against the railings.

"They have to drink each other's saliva to stay alive," I tried to joke. Dodi narrowed her eyes.

"He's an idiot," she announced. "Jake's way nicer."

"Jake's a bit young for Flora," I said.

"I wasn't thinking about Flora," said Dodi.

We all have different reasons for going to the Christmas Extravaganza. Twig is desperate to see the burning slippers and the three little pigs. Zoran says he has always been fascinated by fairy tales, and Jas doesn't want to feel left out. Dad says we have to go because it's culture of a kind, and Mum (who is in Buenos Aires) says we have to go because it's Flora. Even Grandma is coming up from Devon.

Me, I just want to be in the same room as Joss. It's sad, I know, but I just can't help it.

THURSDAY, NOVEMBER 24

I don't know what to think.

Or rather, I do, but I can't believe it. And I don't know how I feel about it. I was right when I wrote that something was up but I never in a million years would have guessed what it was.

I went to the park after school again today with Dodi and the boys. When I came home, the Babes were sitting on their own in the living room with all the lights turned off, eating crisps and watching *Twilight*.

"Zoran put *Madagascar* on," said Jas. "But this is way better."

"He won't mind," said Twig. "Not a single person has died yet."

"Where *is* Zoran?" I asked.

"With Flora," said Jas.

"She's crying," said Twig. "She didn't want to talk to him, but he said he wasn't leaving until she told him what was wrong."

"We're not supposed to know," said Jas.

I didn't really mean to eavesdrop. It just sort of happened, because even though Flora's bedroom door was closed I could hear her inside, sobbing. And then I heard Zoran say things like in the kitchen on Sunday night, like *take responsibility for your actions*, and *it would be best if you came clean and told them*, and Flora sobbing and saying *please don't tell my parents, please don't, please!* And then Zoran saying, really quite passionately, *I will kill that boy with my bare hands*, and Flora crying more quietly and saying *no, Zoran, don't be cross with him, it's my fault*.

My heart was beating like crazy when I looked through the keyhole. Flora was on her beanbag and Zoran was sitting at her desk. I couldn't see his face but I heard him ask her *how are you feeling* and she started to cry again and said *I'm so scared and I feel sick all the time*, and then she threw herself into his arms and he hugged her and she sniffed and said she would be fine and I tiptoed away.

Zoran wouldn't say anything later when I asked him, but I'm not stupid. I've seen *Juno* and read *Dear Nobody* and sat through about a hundred cringe-worthy sex education classes at school. I can guess why she is scared and feels sick all the time.

Flora is going to have a baby.

FRIDAY, NOVEMBER 25

I still can't believe it.

I don't think Joss knows yet. Today I waited on purpose to go to school with them and he didn't seem to treat her any differently from usual. Same arm slung around her shoulders. Same nuzzling. An old lady tutted because they were kissing in the street and Joss just laughed and flipped her off behind her back, which didn't strike me as very prospective parent behavior. I suppose that now we will be linked by ties of blood, which is quite romantic in a hopeless sort of way. Quite honestly I have no idea how Flora managed it. CFS start the whole sex education thing when you're practically still in *primary school*. What we don't know about contraception probably doesn't exist. And of course, I can totally see why teenagers shouldn't have babies. All that dropping out of school and ruined prospects and getting fat and benefit lines. But still—a *baby*! That's just . . . huge. It's *momentous*.

A baby could change *everything*.

I could help look after it. I could take it to the park and to Home Sweet Home to meet Pretty. If it's a girl, and I hope it is, we could call her Poppy or Lily or—no, not Iris. But a flower name, anyway, and a real one, not something stupid like Bluebell.

A baby right, right now would be *perfect*.

I shouldn't have said anything, I know. But when Dodi said *all right then, spill the beans* at lunchtime, I couldn't help it.

"What beans?" I asked.

"You've been completely distracted all morning."

I didn't *really* tell. I said I'd had some big news but it was secret, and then I told them it was family news, and then the boys lost interest but Dodi kept on asking questions until she guessed and said *oh my God Flora's pregnant* and the boys were all *no way* and actually it was really nice to have people looking at me like I had something interesting to say for once. They are sworn to secrecy, of course. *As my friends.* I think I can trust them. I hope so.

I still can't believe it.

Tonight was the opening night of Flora's play.

We all went, like we said we would. We arrived at the theater super early. Flora doesn't like to be interrupted before a show, but I saw Zoran slip backstage and I went after him with the camera. I wanted to film the show, and also people getting ready for it, if they let me. I love that—the craziness of everyone running around half dressed, actors with their hair plastered down ready for their wigs, the pots of thick makeup, stagehands in black tearing around carrying things. It seems completely improbable, half an hour before a show, that it will ever actually happen.

Flora hadn't even started on her makeup. She was leaning against a wall looking quite alarming, waving a dagger in front of her while she listened to Zoran.

"This is not the end of the world," Zoran was saying. "Smile! Try to enjoy it! We'll figure out what to say later."

I crept up and stood by Zoran, but Flora didn't even look at me. She heaved herself off the wall and said she had better get on with things then, even though she would rather walk barefoot on broken glass through a raging blizzard.

"I know what's going on," I blurted. I couldn't help myself. She looked so sad.

"You do?" Flora looked terrified.

"I think it's *brilliant*," I announced, which was only partly

173

true. *Huge* and *momentous* are not the same as *brilliant*, and even though I really was excited, I'm still not sure a baby is a good idea when you're still at school. "I'm really, really happy," I added, because Flora was looking at me like she just couldn't believe her ears.

"You little cow," she spat. She snatched the camera out of my hands. "I should smash this," she snarled. "I should break this on your head!"

"That's enough!" shouted Zoran.

Flora glared at me. I tried to glare back. She turned to Zoran.

"I feel sick," she said.

"Give Blue the camera and go."

Flora went. "What was all that about?" asked Zoran.

"The baby," I mumbled. I couldn't even look at him when I said that but pretended to check my camera for Flora damage instead.

"What baby?"

"You know," I mumbled. I held the camera up to my face. "Flora's."

In the viewfinder, Zoran turned white as a sheet.

And then Joss's friends stumbled in. Their names are CJ, Sharky, and Spudz, and they were waving beer cans and shouting. Julian, who is married to Craig, the Players' director, ran in after them and said they had to leave, but the one called CJ burped in his face and said, "Make me."

Zoran looked dazed and said he'd rather like to find Joss himself, and then Joss turned up looking gorgeous in stage-hand black and said, "Guys!" like them being there was the best thing that could ever have happened in his life and they were all, *We came to see your show and your new girl*, and CJ burped again, and they all hugged and punched each other. And then Flora turned up and cried, "No, you promised!" and the boys were all *so this is the lay-deee* and *man that hair is bad* and Joss had to run after Flora who stormed off, and Julian said we had to go and find our seats *now.*

"What on earth do you mean, Flora's baby?" said Zoran as we walked back to our seats. "And for God's sake put that camera away."

"I heard her telling you." I put the camera down. It's more difficult than it looks to film while walking through a crowded room.

"*What?* When? Wait, here are your parents. Tell me when we're sitting down."

We spent the next few minutes squeezing over people's knees to get to our seats, then squeezing back again because we got the wrong row, then annoying everyone behind us by changing where we were all sitting so that Jas and Twig could see over the people in front. Zoran and I sat at the end of the row. Joss's friends sat a few rows behind us.

"Well?" said Zoran.

Several seats down from us, the parents and Grandma

were poring over the program, looking puzzled.

"In her room. Last Thursday. She was crying."

"Ah," said Zoran.

"I don't understand!" said Dad.

The lights went out.

"What's he talking about?" I asked Zoran.

"Shhh!" said an old lady sitting behind us.

"You'll find out soon enough."

"And what do you mean, *ah*?"

"You'll find that out, too."

"Will you be *quiet*!" hissed the old lady. "My grand-daughter is about to sing."

The Clarendon Players Christmas Extravaganza follows pretty much the same pattern every year. The curtain went up. A choir of primary school children dressed as peasants rejoiced that it was Snow White's birthday. The wicked queen strode on, followed by a girl in a red coat carrying a knife who was meant to be Little Red Riding Hood being the Huntsman. A singing mirror was wheeled onstage, pushed by the Three Little Pigs. Twig, Jas, and all other members of the audience under the age of ten watched with rapt attention.

Zoran looked bemused.

Three rows behind us, Joss's friends started to snore. The old lady behind us hissed at them to be quiet. One of them burped at her.

And then Snow White herself burst on the scene.

I could see why Flora liked her. Snow White is a complete drip normally, but not this one. Craig had set the whole performance in the 1920s, and this Snow White didn't spend her time mooning about with birds and squirrels and baby deer. This Snow White tried on makeup and clothes as she got ready for her party; she minced around in the Wicked Queen's stilettos and made everyone laugh. She lit up the stage, she really did.

Only she wasn't Flora.

Flora came on just before the intermission, dressed as one of the seven dwarfs.

Mum and Dad just about managed to stay in their seats until the intermission, but as soon as the house lights came on again they were up and raring to get backstage.

"I don't think that would be such a good idea," said Zoran. He stood in front of them. He is so slight and they were so determined I was sure they were going to push him out of the way, but Zoran was wearing his *do as I tell you* look and unbelievably they obeyed.

"Something's happened!" cried Mum. "She must be sick!"

"She is not sick," said Zoran.

"There must be some mistake," shouted Dad. "I'm quite sure I remember Flora saying she was playing Snow White."

"There is no mistake," sighed Zoran.

Flora was fired because she kept missing rehearsals. Zoran explained that Craig was going to bar her from the show completely, but then one of the seven dwarfs broke her foot, so he made her do that instead. And he didn't fire Joss because Joss never actually missed any of his run-throughs.

Zoran looked straight ahead as he said all this, like he couldn't quite meet Mum's and Dad's eyes. We all watched with interest as Dad, who is so good with words, struggled to find anything to say at all.

"But you must have noticed!" cried Mum.

"She went almost every night. She just didn't necessarily—get there."

And then all hell broke loose, with this whole torrent of how could this happen and how could you not realize from Mum, and a lot of silence from Dad until she kicked him and he said, we are very disappointed in you, Zoran, because she was your responsibility while we were away. And then Zoran said, with all due respect, she is not my daughter and perhaps you have forgotten, with all your travels, just how difficult it is to manage four children especially when one is a wayward teenager, and Dad said who are you calling wayward and Mum said, well if you feel like that perhaps we should reconsider our arrangement and Zoran said fine, as soon as you find some other poor fool willing to act as cook, babysitter, and surrogate parent he would be on his way. And then Jas wailed NOOOO! and Mum said for heaven's sake Blue can't you go and get them some ice cream or something, but it was too late because the intermission was over.

"She's not pregnant," I said to Zoran as we sat down again. I felt a lot of things right then. Relieved, of course, and stupid, but also sad. Really, really sad.

"Thank heaven for small mercies, eh?" Zoran attempted to smile, but I couldn't smile back.

Without being nasty I have to say that even Flora failed to look good in leather shorts and a pointy hat, but she really did try her best as a dwarf. I'm sure if you didn't know her, and how much she would mind not playing Snow White, you wouldn't have noticed how miserable she looked. Or probably you would just think she was meant to look like that. And it wasn't fair that her clothes were far too small, especially for the Charleston.

Oh, the Charleston.

Snow White's wedding party.

The wicked queen danced, as promised, in a pair of burning slippers (though there was no smell of burning flesh).

Snow White waltzed in her prince's arms.

Little Red Riding Hood strode about in a wolf's pelt. The Three Little Pigs were not, after all, roasted for the feast. Hansel and Gretel turned up with a load of gingerbread, their hearts still beating in their breasts.

The seven dwarfs danced the Charleston.

Nobody should ever dance the Charleston in tight leather shorts. Particularly when they have to end the dance with a forward bend, presenting their bottoms to the audience. Not when there's a chance of the fabric ripping.

Not when the shorts are so tight you couldn't even wear your underwear.

"Well, that was different," said Grandma. "I must come to London more often. It makes such a change from Devon."

Mum and Dad went backstage after the show to find Flora and also to apologize to Craig. The rest of us waited in the foyer. It's amazing how many people from school there were in the audience.

I didn't see the girl until the end, when almost everyone had come out. I found a photograph of her on Joss's Facebook page. You can't mistake her: She has this sharp black bob and green eyes and lots of red lipstick. In the photo she is laughing with another girl who's all fair and wispy and super pretty, but Trudi—that's her name—is the picture of sophistication. When I saw her she was leaning against the wall by the ticket office in a pink leopard-skin coat, and all I could think was how drab everyone looked compared to her.

Flora and Joss appeared just as the last of the audience left the theater. She was crying. He had his arm around her and was trying not to laugh.

"I'll never be able to show my face in public again!" wailed Flora. "My acting career is over!"

Joss started to say *hey, come on, you were fantastic* but then Trudi was peeling herself away from the wall to walk toward them and Flora was saying *who is this* and Joss was looking completely confused.

"What are you doing here?" he asked.

"We have to talk," said Trudi.

"Right," said Joss.

He gave her this look, sort of blank, like he just didn't know what to do. Flora clung to him, but he said he had to go.

"I'll explain later," he said. And then he left with Trudi. Flora cried for him to stay, but he didn't look back.

SATURDAY, DECEMBER 3

Outside the camera, there are no limits. There's you and the person you're with, and the room you are standing in, and outside the room there is the street, and beyond the street there is the town, and beyond the town the countryside, and then there is the sea, and more land, Africa or

Europe or America, and there are more cities and prairies and mountains and cars, and they're all places and people you don't know but which exist anyway. Inside the camera, the world is limited to what you can see through the viewfinder. If you don't like it, you can change it. Or, with the flick of a button, you can switch it off. You just say *good-bye world. Time to go.* Like dying, but not quite so final.

That is why I love it.

SUNDAY, DECEMBER 4 (EARLY MORNING)

Today I am not leaving my room. I hardly left it yesterday either.

It's difficult to know who Mum and Dad are most angry with. At first they kept shouting at Zoran, then Flora leaped to his defense and yelled that at least Zoran was *here*, unlike them, and then the parents started to go on about trust and responsibility and how she has no idea how difficult everything is for them. Then Mum started to cry about how this family was falling apart and how Dad should do something about it, and Dad said Flora wasn't allowed to finish the play and Craig had found another dwarf to replace her. Then when he saw how relieved she was he took away her phone and told her she was grounded.

On and on they went, missing the point.

Grandma left at teatime. Flora went to her room to check her e-mails (she told the parents they can't stop her using her laptop because she needs it for school) and discovered Joss's friends had filmed her Dance of Doom—as Twig calls it—on their phones and posted it on YouTube.

More tears. More tantrums. More *missing the point*.

I went up to my room as soon as dinner was over. I sat by the window. I didn't film, or think, or look at the stars. I literally just sat, and when Joss knocked on the glass I wasn't even surprised.

I opened the window.

"Thanks, Bluebird," said Joss. "Let me in? It's freezing out here."

I didn't let him in. "What are you doing here?" I asked instead.

"Flora's not answering my texts," he said.

"Mum and Dad took her phone."

"That's not very nice of them."

"Flora has seen the YouTube video," I told him. "She says she will never forgive you."

"Yes she will," said Joss. He was so cheerful.

"Who is Trudi?" I asked.

"Trudi," said Joss, "is ancient history."

"She didn't look like ancient history," I said, and Joss said whatever, she was gone now and he wanted to see Flora so please would I go and get her, and I said *no*.

I tried to close the window but he grabbed my wrist.

"Come on, Blue," he smiled. "Don't you want to help us?"

I tried to laugh. I think I wanted to show him that I really couldn't care less about him and Flora but that's not how it came out. My *whatever* laugh sounded more like a sob.

"Blue?"

"It's nothing."

"Blue, look at me."

I did, because I didn't have a choice. He held my chin in his hand and he forced my head back until I looked him in the eyes, and he must have seen that mine were full of tears.

"What's the matter?" he asked.

"It's December third," I told him.

He should have guessed what I was talking about. I know I never told him *when*, but he should have guessed. The old Joss would have. I twisted my head so that my cheek lay against his hand and closed my eyes.

"What's going on, Bluebird?"

I didn't answer. He sighed. Not loudly, but I heard him.

"I really do need to talk to Flora," he whispered.

I shook my head. I didn't watch him go.

Dodi answered her phone on the first ring.

"I miss her," she said, before I even spoke. "I miss her so, so much."

Three years ago last night, Iris left our house, alone.

I was reading *The Hobbit* and didn't want to stop. Dodi was at her house watching the *X Factor* semifinals. It was raining and it was cold and somehow Iris had heard that even though it was winter, and not at all the time for breeding, a vixen had given birth to a litter of cubs under the old shed in the bit of the park where no one is allowed to go, and she had decided we had to rescue them *now*.

"It's so cold!" she pleaded. "They're so little!"

"Their mother will bite us," I said. "We have no idea how to look after baby foxes, the park is locked, it's raining, and I've got to a really good bit in my book."

"IT'S THE SEMIFINAL!" said Dodi when Iris rang her. "And anyway, you know how I feel about wild animals."

Iris hated reading almost as much as she hated the *X-Factor*. She loved animals and she was always in a rush. She never looked where she was going.

We were her almost partners in crime, her faithful lieutenants. We were supposed to look after her.

The florist's van hit her exactly halfway between our two houses, by the entrance to the park.

The driver was distraught.

"I'm sorry," sobbed Dodi on the phone last night.

I hate the stupid Hobbit.

THE FILM DIARIES OF BLUEBELL GADSBY
SCENE THIRTEEN (TRANSCRIPT)
DOOR

DAY. BLUE'S ROOM.

Camera focuses on window, which is half open. Curtains flutter. The sky is the cold pale gray of a London winter.

The door creaks and FLORA tiptoes into the room. She holds her fingers to her lips, opens the window, and slips out. CAMERAMAN (BLUE) sighs and turns. Camera catches feet in a pair of monster slippers, a corner of candy-striped duvet, floor covered in clothes. Cameraman sighs again and slips to the floor. Camera focuses on door and does not move.

Minutes pass, or maybe hours. Door eventually opens, and ZORAN enters.

"Your parents have gone to the park with Jas and Twig," said Zoran. "They thought you were asleep. Where is Flora?"

I pointed at the window. "She went out there," I said. "Hours ago. To see Joss."

Zoran sighed and looked discouraged.

"Three years ago last night," I said, "my twin sister, Iris, was hit by a van."

Zoran sat down next to me on the floor.

"Nobody said anything," I whispered. "They were all too busy shouting at Flora about her stupid play, and *they never said anything.*"

Zoran held my hand.

"Joss Bateman," I said after a while, "is not as lovely as I thought he was," and Zoran said that people rarely are.

"I have only just realized," I said,

"I wish I had known your sister," said Zoran, and I wanted to say "I wish you'd known her, too," except I couldn't speak because my throat hurt. Zoran squeezed my hand harder.

"I have a sister," he said. "But I never see her."

"Why not?" I asked.

"Have I never told you about my family?" asked Zoran, and I said no, and he said it's a sad story and I said well, today is a day for sad stories.

So then Zoran told me how when he was six years old his parents traveled through their country, which was at war, all the way from the town where they lived to the coast, where they put him and his sister on a boat.

"To England? All the way from Bosnia?"

"To Italy, and then we took a train. We were lucky, we had passports and some money and Alina's address in Putney to give to anyone who asked us. My sister was older than me; she spoke a little English."

"Why didn't your parents go, too?"

"They meant to, but then there wasn't enough room for them on the boat, or rather not enough money to pay for them, too. They said they would come after us. That was the story at the time. Looking back on it, I think they always knew we would be going alone."

I had a vision then of a young Zoran crying on a rickety old ferry, with every deck crammed full of people trying to catch one last look at their loved ones on the quayside, and six-year-old Zoran waving to his mother with his big sister standing beside him holding his hand. In my head the sky was blue and the sun was hot and there were gulls circling overhead. The boat pushed away from the quay and everyone was crying and the people on the quayside were growing smaller and smaller, including Zoran's mother whose heart was breaking into a million little pieces even though she was waving back and smiling.

"You never saw her again," I said.

"No," said Zoran. "I didn't."

"How did they die?"

"I don't know."

"And your sister?"

"She went back after the war. She is married to a Bosnian man; they have two sons and she works as a pediatric nurse. She was always good at looking after people. She doesn't like to come to England because it reminds her of leaving our parents. And I don't like to go to Bosnia, for the same reason. Sometimes we meet up in Paris."

We stayed there, not talking again, and I thought of his parents doing what they thought was right for their children, and his sister helping children who were sick, and then I thought of Iris.

"It seems to me, Blue, that you are lost," said Zoran after a while. "And yet also that you do not wish to be found."

Zoran and his cryptic comments.

"You should go and see her," I said. "Your sister."

"Maybe I will, soon," said Zoran.

"What's her name?" I asked.

"Lena," he said. "My sister's name is Lena."

I started to cry then. Zoran put his arms around me.

We sat there for ages not talking, and the tears just kept on coming, as together we watched the light outside my window fade from gray to blue then black.

THE FILM DIARIES OF BLUEBELL GADSBY
SCENE FOURTEEN (TRANSCRIPT)
THE LECTURE

NIGHT. THE ENTIRE GADSBY CLAN IS GATHERED
IN THE LIVING ROOM. THE BLUE CURTAINS WITH
THE UNFINISHED EMBROIDERY ARE DRAWN. A
COAL FIRE BURNS IN THE GRATE.

FLORA sits ramrod straight and stiff in the low
green velvet chair. JAS and TWIG sit squeezed
together on the sofa, with ZORAN beside them
looking unhappy. MOTHER and FATHER stand side
by side on the hearth rug. Mother's eyes are red.
Father looks uncomfortable.

> FATHER
> (apologetically)
> Blue, we would rather you didn't film right now.

> (picture wobbles as CAMERAMAN shrugs)

MOTHER

(in a low voice, speaking very fast and looking
at the fire)

This has been a difficult time for all of us. We're
not angry and your father and I want you to
know we love you very much, and we both hate
being away from home so much.

FLORA

Don't do it then. Nobody's forcing you.

MOTHER

(ignoring Flora)

Friday night's fiasco has made us realize that
things are getting out of hand. They can't carry
on like this.

We need some ground rules.

FATHER

(clearly reciting a list they prepared earlier)

Twig and Jas: no running off to school on your
own. Blue: no skateboarding in the park at night.
Zoran is to know where you all are *at all times*.
Flora, no hanging around with the boy next door.

FLORA

Oh for God's sake.

MOTHER

He's clearly a bad influence.

FATHER

(doggedly)

This family will learn to behave as a proper
family again! That means eating meals together!
Walking to school together! Being there for each
other!

JAS

(hopefully)

Does that mean you're going to live at home
again?

FLORA

(viciously)

Or are you hoping to enforce these laws by
Skype?

(Mother looks like she might cry.)

FATHER

Zoran will be here to make sure you behave.

ZORAN

Actually, yesterday you fired me.

JAS

NOOOOOOO!

MOTHER

Dear Zoran, about that . . .

(Doorbell rings. Mother hurries from room to

answer it.)

FATHER

Who the devil? On a Sunday night?

(Mother returns, looking perplexed)

MOTHER

Apparently you ordered a piano?

THE FILM DIARIES OF BLUEBELL GADSBY
SCENE FIFTEEN (TRANSCRIPT)
THE PIANO

EVENING. STILL IN THE LIVING ROOM, WHICH IS
NOW A MESS OF FURNITURE PULLED AWAY FROM
THE WALL TO MAKE ROOM FOR AN UPRIGHT
PIANO, THE OLD-FASHIONED KIND WITH CANDLE-
HOLDERS AND KEYS SO OLD THEY ARE NOT
WHITE BUT YELLOW, WHICH STANDS WHERE THE
SOFA USED TO BE.

The GADSBY family, plus ZORAN but minus BLUE
who is holding the camera, crowd around the piano in
varying states of disbelief.

>   MOTHER
>   Remind me again why . . .

>   FATHER
>   It was a surprise for Blue! She wanted a piano!!
>   I forgot!!!

FLORA

Blue? A piano? Since when?

JAS

I have always *longed* to play the piano!

FLORA

Actually, come to think of it, I'd quite like to as
well.

MOTHER

But who will teach you? I don't have time to find
a piano teacher!

CAMERAMAN (BLUE)

Zoran will teach me.

FLORA, FATHER, and MOTHER

Zoran?

CAMERAMAN (BLUE)

Show them, Zoran.

Zoran approaches the piano with diffidence, conscious
of everyone's eyes upon him. Mother and Father look
bewildered, Jas and Twig excited, Flora sarcastic.

ZORAN

Beethoven. *Moonlight Sonata.*

He plays. Mother and Father fall as one onto the sofa
and stare. The Babes' jaws drop open. Flora begins
to smile. Zoran goes on to play something by Chopin,
moves on to the Beatles (inevitably, "Hey Jude"), and
shimmies on to a special Zoran piano remix of Jack
Johnson's "Banana Pancakes," the Babes' favorite song
of the moment. He sings. They sing, too. Even Flora
joins in. Mother and Father begin to smile. Father
holds out his arms and Mother leans back into them
with feigned reluctance. He draws her toward him and
kisses the side of her head. She looks away, her eyes
suspiciously bright, but she moves closer to him. Her
right foot starts to beat in time to the music and she
begins to sing.

MONDAY, DECEMBER 5

Zoran understands. How is it my family doesn't?

I left them to their singing last night and came up to
my room to get some peace. I lay on my bed and used
the camera to focus on the glow-in-the-dark stars on the
ceiling. They freaked me out at first but Iris loved them, so

I brought them with me when I moved. Downstairs, they were back on the Beatles, with Zoran thumping out "All You Need Is Love" and them all belting it out, even Mum and Dad, and I thought, is that really all it takes to make them forget? A piano appears and they turn into the family von Trapp?

Mum came up. Flushed from singing but wearing a serious expression and carrying a mug of tea.

"I brought you some chocolate biscuits as well," she said.

She put the mug on my bedside table together with the biscuits. I filmed the ceiling, hoping she would leave, but she just stood at my window watching the rain.

"You were singing," I said at last. "Yesterday was the third of December and you didn't say anything and today you were *singing*."

She turned away from the window. I carried on filming the ceiling.

"Look at me, Blue," whispered Mum. "Look at me *really*, not hiding behind your camera. Look at me and tell me it doesn't hurt me every bit as much as it hurts you."

"You were singing," I repeated, still filming the ceiling. "And I would like you to leave."

She stopped at the door on her way out.

"Happiness is a choice, Blue," she said. "Sometimes it's the hardest choice we have to make."

When Mum was gone, I picked up the mug of tea. It was

exactly how I like it, hot and milky and very sweet.

Exactly how Iris liked it.

I drank it all, down to the very last drop.

Then I threw the mug against the wall and smashed it.

I couldn't care less about the parents' stupid new rules.

Today I marched up to Jake as soon as I got to school and told him that I wanted him to teach me to skate.

"Properly," I said. "Tonight. After school."

"WOO-HOO!" said Tom. "I'm up for it."

"Not you," I hissed. "Just him. And I'll need your board."

"DOUBLE WOO-HOO!" said Tom. Jake and I both silenced him with a glare.

It was totally different tonight. Usually, when we all go together, the boys are joking and messing about, but Jake and I hardly spoke. We got to the park and he asked, very quietly, what I wanted to do.

"I want to learn to fly," I told him.

"Right," said Jake.

I stood in the middle of the park, staring up at the ramps. I pushed myself off, making straight for one of them, trying to gather enough speed to go up it, and I slid straight back down again.

"Not like that," said Jake. "Watch me."

He showed me how to rock sideways, each time going a

little higher up the ramps, gathering speed. I fell off, but before he could ask if I'd hurt myself I tried again. Backward and forward, higher and higher, falling, hurting, getting up, until by the time it was almost dark I was bruised all over but soaring to the top of each ramp and whooshing back down and up the other side. I was cold when I started, but each time I fell I shed another layer and each time I got back on I felt lighter and went higher, hair flying, the night wind whipping my face.

Jake said it was time for a break and we sat with our backs against the ramp, sharing a Snickers he pulled out of his bag.

"Iris would have loved skateboards," I said. "In fact, I'm surprised she never tried."

"Is that what this is all about?" asked Jake. He wasn't looking at me when he said it, but straight ahead at the ramp opposite.

"Mum says happiness is a choice," I told him. "And Zoran says I'm lost but don't want to be found."

"You're here now, though," Jake said.

Our feet were almost touching. I jumped up and grabbed my board.

"I'm going to try and flip," I said.

"I'm not sure you're ready for that," he called, but I was already away.

Jake was wrong, I was ready for it. All I'd done this

afternoon was go up and down the ramps, faster and faster, but this time I flew off the top. Literally, I flew. It didn't last long but there was a moment which felt like forever when the board left the ground and I was just floating, and then I managed to twist, and the board hit the ground with a jolt which went straight up my spine, and I skidded down the ramp on my tummy and lay at the bottom in a heap, with everything hurting, and I laughed. I laughed until I had cramps in my tummy and my eyes were streaming and even I couldn't tell anymore if I was laughing or crying.

When I finally stopped, Jake was standing beside me.

"That was brilliant," he said. He held out his hands to help me to my feet and smiled. "That was totally brilliant."

For a moment, standing there in the dark with the wind rustling the trees and the whole park to ourselves, we looked at each other like we had never seen each other before.

"Brilliant," repeated Jake. And then we left the park, carrying our boards.

THURSDAY, DECEMBER 8

Mum and Dad have been away all week, and despite their rules Zoran isn't even trying to stop Flora from seeing Joss. This might be because at the moment, she is the only happy person in the house. She was practically singing when she climbed back through my window on Sunday. Apparently Trudi is not Joss's girlfriend like we all thought, or even his ex-girlfriend, but the best friend of a girl called Kiera he used to go out with in Guildford. (Kiera is the other girl in the photograph on his Facebook page, the fair wispy pretty one.) He dumped her when he left Guildford, and she sent Trudi to London to tell him she wants him back, but Joss said no, because he loves Flora. Also, he agreed that his friends had been completely out of order, and he yelled at them on the phone and threatened never to speak to them again unless they took the video down.

Today I came home from school to find Jas and Twig Skyping Dad in the kitchen.

"I would *not* like to live in a medieval castle," Jas was saying. "Medieval castles are drafty and broken."

"Well, obviously *now* they're broken," Dad said. It's always quite funny to see him on Skype. He sits much too close to the screen and looks like an alien. "In medieval times, they were quite different. Twig?"

"It would depend on the castle." Twig wasn't really paying attention, because he was trying to do his science homework at the same time as talking to Dad. Twig has had so many notes about overdue homework he could bind them together and make quite a thick book.

"But if you were a princess," said Dad, sounding desperate. "If you didn't have a choice and *had* to live in a castle but could have anything you wanted there, what would that be?"

"If I could have anything I wanted," Jas said, looking very prim, "it would be to have all my family around me."

I have never seen an alien look so depressed.

FRIDAY, DECEMBER 9

Tom Myers, that loudmouth, has told the entire school that Flora is going to have a baby.

Tom says *but I only told my sister,* like he doesn't understand that's not the point, which is that when something is secret, you don't tell *anybody.* His sister probably only told one person, too. Who told someone else, who told someone else, until everybody knew except the people concerned. Who found out in the canteen when that idiot Graham Lewis bounced up to them making baby noises.

"Oh my God!" cried Flora. "Are you saying I look fat?"

"Mama!" said Graham, cracking up. "Dada!"

Joss laughed his head off when he understood what Graham meant. "Mate," he said to Graham (who told everyone who wanted to listen), "mate, you and me need to have a little conversation about the facts of life."

Normally boys want people to think that they are doing loads more things with girls than they actually are, but Joss didn't seem to care. Graham said, "What, really, never?" and Joss just laughed harder and said in a jokey sort of way, "Not for lack of trying, mate," and Flora went bright red and looked like she might murder Graham and throw his body to ravening vultures.

It took her about twenty seconds to work out that the source of the rumor was me. I tried to apologize but she didn't listen. "I don't know what's got into you lately," she fumed, and "I used to like having you as a sister and maybe one day when I forget what it feels like to be HUMILIATED in front of the WHOLE FREAKING SCHOOL I might forgive you."

Joss was still laughing all the time she was yelling at me, so then she turned on him and started screaming at him about how insensitive and immature he was being.

"Just because I've got a sense of humor," said Joss, and Flora said, "What is that supposed to mean," and Joss said, "Lighten up can't you," and suddenly they were in the middle of an argument and didn't notice me tiptoeing away.

THE FILM DIARIES OF BLUEBELL GADSBY
SCENE SIXTEEN (TRANSCRIPT)
IN GERMANY THEY DECORATE THEIR TREES
ON CHRISTMAS EVE

THE LANDING OUTSIDE FATHER'S STUDY

From behind the closed door, the sound of battle
cries and loud music. TWIG and JAS jostle each
other, looking anxious.

> TWIG
> You go.

> JAS
> No, you.

> TWIG
> No, you.

> FATHER'S VOICE
> (from within study)

Whatever you want, go away! I am trying to work
in here!

(Twig takes a deep breath and throws open the study
door.)

TWIG
We would like to go and buy a Christmas tree.

FATHER sits at his desk, reams of paper spread out
before, around, and behind him. Light flickers from
his open laptop. Music and the sound of battle grow
louder.

FATHER
(not looking up)
Well off you go, then.

JAS
We need you to come with us.

FATHER
Where's your mother?

JAS
She is still jet-lagged from Argentina.

FATHER

What about Zoran? Don't I pay him for things
like this?

BLUE'S VOICE

He has gone to visit Alina in her nursing home.

FATHER

Who on earth is Alina?

JAS

Please, Daddy? You're only watching a film.

FATHER

I am not watching a film, I am working. One
day when you are older, you will understand.
In Germany they decorate their trees on
Christmas Eve. In Russia, not until the New
Year. Now go.

JAS

(bursts into tears)

I hate you, Daddy!

FATHER

(roaring from behind study door, which has
slammed shut)

And I hate ****** Christmas!

THE FILM DIARIES OF BLUEBELL GADSBY
SCENE SEVENTEEN (TRANSCRIPT)
THE POINT IS, WE DON'T ACTUALLY LIVE IN GERMANY

AFTERNOON. THE GADSBY LIVING ROOM. A COAL
FIRE BURNS ONCE AGAIN IN THE GRATE.

FLORA sits on the chaise longue in the farthest corner of the room IMing Tamsin about her argument
with Joss. FATHER sits asleep in an armchair by the
fire, the Sunday papers spilling off his lap. MOTHER,
TWIG, and JAS sit around the coffee table, playing
Monopoly and eating a chocolate and pistachio torte
prepared earlier by ZORAN. Mother hates Monopoly
but is taking part in a show of family unity. Twig loves
Monopoly but his heart isn't in it. You can tell by the
way he stares into space. Jas is compensating for this
by being extra polite.

MOTHER

I must say, darlings, this cake is quite delicious.
Did you help Zoran make it?

JAS

I'm so glad you like it, Mummy. Twig! Do pay
attention, I am about to buy the whole of Mayfair.

TWIG

The point is, we don't actually live in Germany.

MOTHER

Well no, darling, but she said Mayfair.

TWIG

Which means that *we* always get our Christmas
tree at the beginning of December.

JAS

Shh, Daddy'll hear.

FATHER

(waking up)

Daddy'll hear what?

TWIG

Even when Iris was in hospital. And now it is the
end of the second weekend in December.

FATHER

Even when Iris was in hospital what?

TWIG

WE HAD A TREE AT THE BEGINNING OF
DECEMBER! AND WE DO NOT LIVE IN GERMANY!

Father's response is muffled by a door opening. Zoran
enters and comes to stand in the middle of the room.
He grips a fur hat in his hands, and even though he
speaks to Mother he does not look at her. This has the
effect of making him look like a Russian peasant come
to beg a favor.

ZORAN

I have news I am afraid you will not like.

MOTHER

(gushing, trying to make up for the fact that just
a week ago she tried to fire him)
Oh, Zoran, I'm sure it can't be that bad!

ZORAN

The thing is, my great-aunt is getting married.

SUNDAY, DECEMBER 11

So Zoran's fears have been confirmed, and Alina has accepted Peter's proposal.

"Did you tell her he is just in it for the money?" I asked.

"What!" cried Mum. "Blue! What do you know about this?"

"I went to visit one day when I didn't go to school."

"What I don't understand," grumbled Dad, "is why you think *we* will not like this news?"

Zoran explained that Alina is getting married tomorrow and that she has decided to go to Paris on her honeymoon. Paris is where she went on her first honeymoon, he said, and she has very fond memories of it. Only because this time she and her fiancé are so old, she wants Zoran to go with them. Just in case something goes wrong, she says. I could tell Dad was dying to ask *what sort of thing* but Mum shook her head and he didn't.

"My sister will also be in Paris." Zoran looked at me when he said that. "She is coming from Sarajevo with her family."

"But when will you be back?" cried Mum.

"I don't know," said Zoran, and we all had to lean forward

to hear him. He wasn't looking at any of us now, but straight out of the window. "I haven't seen her for a very long time."

"You're leaving?" Jas's eyes were huge and her lower lip began to wobble.

"But you can't!" Mum was almost crying, too. "I'm due in New York on Tuesday!"

I don't think I've ever seen anyone look so sad and so determined at the same time. Zoran said that he was very sorry and Alina had only just remembered to tell him. He said that she was ninety-five years old and very forgetful and the whole thing was decided in rather a hurry.

"But *why* such a rush?" cried Dad.

"She is ninety-five years old," repeated Zoran.

"He means, she might drop dead at any minute," explained Flora.

"Quite," said Zoran.

"Oh," said Dad.

"I don't suppose you could work from home this week, David?" asked Mum.

"Alina would like you to film the wedding," Zoran told me. "It will be in Richmond, at the local church."

"Absolutely not!" said Dad.

Zoran looked confused.

"Tell me, David," said Mum. "Exactly what *is* keeping you in Warwick now that term has ended?"

"I can't concentrate anywhere else," said Dad. "I have

reached a critical stage of my new project. You will simply have to tell Bütylicious that you can't go to New York."

There was no getting any sense out of either of them after that. We all slunk down to the kitchen where Zoran made us fried peanut butter and banana sandwiches.

"Perhaps your grandmother can come and stay," he said, but none of us answered. In the end, Flora just said, "I can't believe you're leaving us," and he said, "I'm sorry," and then nobody spoke for a while and Zoran said he had to go and pack.

"Do you think," Twig asked when he had gone, "we are actually going to have Christmas this year?"

Jas slipped across the room and put her hand in mine. "What about Christmas Eve?" she whispered.

The parents' voices floated down the stairs. "Point of information, David!" we heard Mum shout. "Being a father does entail *some* responsibilities!"

"Look who's talking!" Dad bellowed. "Look who's flitting off to bloody New York again!"

"I am not flitting!" screamed Mum. "And I don't have a choice!"

"Well neither do I!" hollered Dad.

Flora said we should definitely prepare ourselves for the worst. She said more couples split up at Christmas than at any other time of year.

Upstairs, Mum started to cry.

THE FILM DIARIES OF BLUEBELL GADSBY
SCENE EIGHTEEN
WEDDING

PART 1:

INSIDE ST. CLEMENT'S CHURCH, RICHMOND

Pale sunlight streams through the high windows, glinting on rows of blue-rinsed hair and walkers. The church is packed.

The organ strikes up a wedding march. The congregation whispers excitedly. At the front, PETER rises unsteadily to his feet and leans heavily on his walking stick. ALINA enters the church on ZORAN's arm. She wears a lavender suit, a matching pillbox hat with a little purple veil, and a radiant smile. She walks slowly. For an awful moment, when she lets go of Zoran's arm at the top of the aisle, it looks as though she might fall, but he dashes forward to steady her. Chin high, she turns to greet her groom.

PRIEST steps forward to take them by the hand and invites them to sit in the two carved chairs before the altar. Then he looks up at the camera and indicates it should be switched off.

PART 2

INSIDE THE RETIREMENT HOME

White balloons float above the curtain rods of the lounge. Silver streamers curl down. A Christmas tree twinkles in the corner, and fairy lights have been strung across the mantelpiece. An enormous bouquet of lilies adorns a trestle table, heaving under the weight of a buffet. Residents of the home, in varying stages of intoxication, guzzle sparkling wine and cocktail sausages. Care workers circulate among them, topping off glasses and dishing out more food. Zoran sits at the piano, playing ragtime tunes. Alina sits beside Peter on the sofa, clutching his hand. Peter leans forward and kisses her gently on the cheek. She turns to look at him. There are tears in her eyes. He reaches out to stroke her face. She puts her head on his shoulder. He smiles and closes his eyes.

They look as though they may have fallen asleep, but they also look happy.

Everyone looks happy.

TUESDAY, DECEMBER 13

The parents' argument on Sunday lasted well into the night. Dad went back to Warwick yesterday; Zoran went to Paris with Alina; and Grandma came up from Devon. Mum left for New York this morning.

We watched her go from Flora's bedroom window. She didn't want to wake us, she said last night when she kissed us all good-bye, but the amount of noise she made with the shower and hauling her case downstairs, she would have woken a hibernating sloth (if sloths hibernated, which Twig says they don't). The Babes went into Flora's room first, dragging their duvets, and after a while I pulled my own duvet off the bed and scurried across the landing to join them. I wasn't sure if Flora would let me into her room, but she didn't say anything.

It is almost midwinter and it was still pitch-dark outside. The taxi driver waited for Mum in the street and you could see his breath coming out in little puffs of steam which turned orange in the glow of the streetlamp. She kept checking her bag and looking back at the house and adjusting her coat and gloves. Jas said, do you think maybe she won't go, but then Mum squared her shoulders and did that head shake thing she does when she's made her mind up about something, and the next thing she was in the taxi and driving down the street and we were all feeling slightly sick from getting up so early.

The first person I saw at school this morning was Jake.

"I went to an old people wedding," I told him when he asked where I was yesterday, and then I said, "I think it was the sweetest thing I've ever seen in my life," because it's true. I can't stop thinking about Alina and how peaceful she looked, sitting with her head on Peter's shoulder, and how proud he looked to have her there. Even Zoran relented when he was bringing me home after the wedding, and said that Peter's intentions toward Alina probably are honorable after all. He says it helps that Alina has made it very clear to Peter that when she dies all her wordly goods will go to Zoran and his sister.

"Why was it so sweet?" asked Jake.

"Because they were so happy," I said. "It makes a nice change in my life, believe me."

Jake put his arm around my shoulders and hugged me. It felt nice. I thought about Alina and put my head on his shoulder, just to see what it was like. It hurt my neck a bit, but I liked it.

And then Joss walked past.

All he did was wave. Well, wave, then raise his eyebrows and look from me to Jake and back again, and grin like he was saying *really? You two?* We both saw it. Jake dropped his arm and I jumped away. I felt myself go bright red. We started to walk toward the science block and Jake said, "You really like him, don't you?"

"No way," I said.

Jake looked unconvinced.

"He's Flora's boyfriend!" I said.

Jake shrugged.

"I don't know," I said at last. Jake smiled at that, and punched me lightly on the arm.

"You can't help who you like," he said. He walked off ahead of me to join the others, then turned to see if I was following and smiled again. I thought, he looks exactly the same as he did when he tried to kiss me behind the toilets when we were eight. He has the same light brown eyes, the same messy chestnut hair, the same skinny body, except somehow despite being the same he is also different. I thought, I wish you could help who you like.

I managed to speak to Mum on the phone this evening. She was in a taxi, she said, on her way to her first meeting. I could hear the sound of traffic and car horns in the background.

"Is it possible," I asked her, "to love and hate someone at the same time?"

"Are you talking about your father?" she asked.

"Do you love and hate Daddy?"

"I love him," said Mum, "but he drives me crazy. Who are you talking about?"

"It doesn't matter. So you do think it's possible?"

Mum said that she thinks love and hate are similar emotions. She said that both could be passionate and obsessive, and that each could turn into the other very easily. She said that she thought you *could* love and hate at the same time, but that surely it was better to love, didn't I think?

"Hmm," I said.

Mum said she had to go because she had arrived at her meeting.

"What are we going to do for Christmas?" I asked.

"Oh, sweetie!" she said. "Something nice, I promise. Something special."

And with that, she was gone.

WEDNESDAY, DECEMBER 14

Joss had a half day yesterday and I know he went to Guildford to see Kiera. I know because his mates couldn't wait to start posting about it. They don't like Flora because she was so cross after the YouTube thing, and they say that they never see Joss anymore because of her. He's deleted their comments now, but I know Flora also knows because she looks terrible. Her eyes are red and she isn't wearing any makeup and she is wandering around in leggings and an old gray cardigan of Dad's, which is not a good look for someone with multicolored hair.

Flora knows that I know about Kiera because she caught me looking at Joss's Facebook page. She said that she supposes I am pleased. "I suppose you consider this some sort of victory," is what she actually said, and when I didn't answer she went, "Oh stop pretending; we all know you're jealous."

"You're so not worth it," I mumbled.

"Joss loves me," she said, like she was trying to convince herself. "This Kiera girl is nothing. He's told me. He just went to see her because he feels sorry for her. He loves *me*."

"I can't think why!" I yelled as she crossed the landing from my room back to hers. "When you're such a cow!"

We never used to be so horrible to each other.

I realize now that I will never be as important to Joss as he is to me. To him, I am his girlfriend's funny little sister, whom he once helped out for a laugh and maybe also to impress Flora. I know he isn't as lovely as I thought he was. The way he looked at me and Jake, like somehow he had a right to comment, as if he was *entitled*—I didn't like that.

And yet, I can't help it. Yesterday when I saw him my heart thumped and it felt like it dropped right into my boots and bounced straight back up again.

FRIDAY, DECEMBER 16

Being with Grandma in London is quite different from being with Grandma in Devon. I'm not sure she knows how to manage us here.

Flora came home in a rage today. Rumor has finally caught up with the teaching staff at Clarendon Free School, and today Anthea Foundry told Flora that she must feel absolutely free to confide in her *about anything*. She said she knew a *lot* of girls who had had babies *very* young, and that she was *completely nonjudgmental*.

"It was the most embarrassing experience of my entire life!" Flora screamed at me. "And I've had a *lot* of humiliating experiences recently!"

And then Grandma tried not to look shocked when Flora said I told everyone she was having a baby, and Flora had to explain it wasn't true and Grandma got very confused and asked, if it wasn't true, why did I tell everyone? And I had to explain about eavesdropping and getting it all wrong, and by the time I finished I was almost crying and Jas came in and said she was sorry to disturb us but could we go and buy a Christmas tree? "And can we also," said Jas, because Grandma didn't answer, "can we also make gingerbread cookies and ice them to make decorations? And make our own Christmas cards? Can we go ice-skating, and can we get a puppy?"

Jas has started speaking in this baby voice, and it is really, really annoying.

"Of course, darling." Grandma got her voice back, and Jas looked up like she couldn't believe her ears. "Except the puppy," said Grandma quickly. "I'm not sure your parents could cope with a puppy."

Twig came in from the garden with Betsy or Petal and said, do you think she's getting fat, and Grandma became a bit more Grandma-like and yelled NO RATS IN THE KITCHEN so loudly he dropped Petal or Betsy and we spent ages trying to catch her again, except Flora who was at Joss's because she is determined to spend as much time as possible showing him how much nicer she is than Kiera.

"Just in case," I heard her tell Tamsin on the phone.

It is almost ten thirty. Grandma keeps trying to make the Babes go to bed, but she burned the first batch of cookies because the thermostat on the oven is broken, and Jas says she won't go to sleep until they've finished all the icing.

SUNDAY, DECEMBER 18

Dad didn't come home this weekend. Grandma shouted at him. Mum called to say she is in Boston. Joss has gone home to Guildford for the holidays. Flora is moping.

TUESDAY, DECEMBER 20

Twig spent the morning searching all the wardrobes and drawers and cupboards in the house and announced that this is not how Christmas is supposed to be.

"At Christmas," said Twig, "there should be presents hidden all over the place."

"Mummy should be here," said Jas. "Getting stressed about the cooking."

I didn't say anything. I have my own views about Christmas.

Grandma is trying to re-create Devon, in terms of busyness I mean. On Sunday she sent us ice-skating at Somerset House, and told us to get the bus up Regent Street and Oxford Street to look at the Christmas lights.

"I WANT PHOTOGRAPHS," she said. "TO PROVE YOU'VE DONE IT."

Flora grumbled that it was the sort of thing only people who don't live in London do, but Grandma was adamant.

Yesterday she made us go to Winter Wonderland in Hyde Park, which Flora said was even more touristy than the lights. Flora took us up the Power Tower, which is like a giant elevator you sit on which hoists you up to the top of a 66-meter tower before dropping you down to the ground again. Jas threw up and Flora lost her wallet so we had to walk home through Hyde Park and Kensington Gardens in the dark. It was so cold my nostrils were sticking together.

Today we finally bought our tree. It is so big it doesn't actually fit in the living room. We have put it in the hall, and we ran up and down the stairs all afternoon to decorate it. Flora skulked around the landing barking orders at us and behaving almost like her normal bossy self.

WEDNESDAY, DECEMBER 21

Zoran e-mailed us today. He sent photographs of Peter and Alina enjoying their honeymoon in Paris. Mainly they seemed to be in restaurants, but there was one of the two of them sitting on a park bench in front of the Eiffel Tower, all wrapped up in coats and hats and shawls. She has her head on his shoulder and his eyes are closed, but his smile couldn't be any wider.

"Aren't they sweet?" wrote Zoran. "Don't they look happy?"

He wrote that Alina is knitting Peter a new cardigan for Christmas. She started knitting it before the wedding, which she says in the old days would have been plenty of time but now is a cause for concern, seeing as she has arthritis in all her fingers and her eyes are so bad. The cardigan is a strange shape and also a very odd mix of colors, but Peter says it doesn't matter, he can just wrap it around his neck when it gets drafty.

There was another photograph, of a man and two boys and a woman who looks so much like Zoran she could only be his sister.

"We have decided to spend Christmas in Paris," wrote Zoran. "Lena wanted us all to go back to Sarajevo with her, but Alina can't travel that far. Lena says, and she is right, that the important thing at Christmas is to be with people you love."

"Surely," Flora frowned, "he loves us, too?"

Jas said how nice it was that Alina and Peter were so in love, and that she hopes when Mum and Dad are old they will be just like that, and Flora said "as if that is ever going to happen" and then Jas cried, and Grandma got really cross and asked Flora why she has to say things like that when she knows how sensitive Jas is, and Flora burst into tears, too.

Flora ditched Joss today, in response to comments on his wall that Joss Bateman thinks there's no place like home and Spudz always knew that Guildford girls do it better even though that girl with the mad hair does have a lovely bottom.

Flora waited about five minutes for Joss to leap to her defense (I know, because I was watching the conversation) and then she jumped in and wrote, *you are all a bunch of immature idiots and that includes you, Joss Bateman.*

CJ wrote, *Woo-hoo!*

Flora wrote, *butt out, CJ, this is none of your business.*

Sharky wrote, *butt out! BUTT!! Get it??? BUTT!!! BUTT!!!!*

Flora wrote, *oh, grow up*

Spudz wrote, *she's got a nice arse but zero sense of humor.*

Then the phone rang and it was Joss, and I don't know what he said to her but it was impossible not to hear what Flora said to him, which was basically WAS HE SEEING KIERA AGAIN and HOW COULD SHE KNOW HE WAS TELLING THE TRUTH and HIS FRIENDS HAD NO RESPECT FOR HER AND SHE WAS NOT HYSTERICAL. And then she yelled that she hated him and didn't want to see him again, ever, and burst into tears.

Flora cried all day. She tried to call Mum, but her phone

was switched off, which made her cry even more, and it didn't help when Grandma reminded her that it was only six o'clock in the morning in New York.

"I'm going to call Dad," said Flora, still crying. "At least one of my parents has to answer."

But Dad's phone just rang and rang, and Flora cried even harder.

It's snowing in Scotland. Every time we switch on the radio, we hear about how people in the Highlands are only surviving by keeping shovels with them at all times to dig themselves out of snowdrifts.

"I wish it would snow here," said Jas.

Grandma made soup with cheese on toast and mince pies for pudding. We watched *It's a Wonderful Life*, like we do every Christmas. Flora came down with her duvet and a very red nose. We all pretended everything was fine, but just now Twig came into my room and sat cross-legged on the floor, watching me while I write.

"This is going to be a rubbish Christmas," he said.

"Yup," I said.

"Do you miss her?" he asked.

"Who?" I asked.

"Don't pretend," he said.

"Well what do you think?"

"I think you do only you never say so. *Nobody* ever says so. It's not right."

My little brother, growing up.

"Of course I miss her," I said. "Every day. I miss the parents, too."

"I wish they'd come home," he said.

He stayed for ages while I wrote, sitting with his head against my bed, staring at the door. He only got up to leave when I told him I wanted to go to sleep.

"I'll get them back," he said before he left my room. "Somehow. I will."

And then he was gone.

FRIDAY, DECEMBER 23

It snowed in the night. I knew as soon as I woke up. The light in my room was different, pale and filtered, and there was no sound from outside at all. I jumped out of bed and drew the curtains and sure enough, the world had disappeared under a thick carpet of white. It was freezing. I pulled on a sweatshirt and some socks and ran next door to tell Twig and Jas.

They weren't in their room, so I went down to the kitchen. Flora was sitting slumped at the breakfast counter looking miserable, and Grandma, looking long-suffering, was making toast.

"Is everything okay?" I asked.

Flora slumped even lower.

"Something about Facebook," said Grandma.

"What's happened now?" I asked.

"What do you care!" Flora cried, and she ran out of the room.

Grandma looked baffled. Suddenly I really, really missed Zoran. If he was here, I thought, I would tell him about my solo skateboarding session with Jake, about how it felt like flying. I thought how Zoran, who has never liked Joss, probably would like Jake.

And then it started. I asked, "Where are the Babes?" and Grandma said, "In bed, go and get them up, they shouldn't miss this," and I said, "They're not in bed, I just checked," and Grandma said, "Well they're not down here." And then I thought they might be in the garden, but the door was locked, and Grandma thought they might be upstairs watching TV, but they weren't, and then Flora stopped crying and joined in and we looked everywhere, including the loft and the cellar, but there was no sign of them. And then Grandma noticed that their coats and boots had gone, as well as all the ginger cookies from the tree and all the housekeeping money. And I remembered Twig last night saying "I'll get them back."

"Oh my God," cried Flora when I told her. "The Babes have run away!"

Grandma went white and said that no, they had probably gone to the park to build a snowman.

"There are no footprints outside!" shouted Flora. "They must have gone out ages ago!"

"GO AND LOOK FOR THEM!" yelled Grandma. "RUN! WHILE I CALL THE POLICE!"

So Flora and I pulled on snow boots and anoraks over our pajamas and we ran out into the street, and as we ran we phoned everyone we know, Jake and Dodi and all of Flora's friends, to ask them if they could help us look, but I knew and Flora knew that it was pointless. And we were right. By the time we finished searching there were loads of us scouring the park, and the Babes weren't there.

Jake and Dodi came home with us, and when we got back we found Grandma on the doorstep talking to a policeman named Officer Roberts. He was very short, had a moustache, and looked very unhappy.

"YOU MUST DO SOMETHING!" boomed Grandma. "YOU MUST INSTIGATE A NATIONAL SEARCH!"

"But do you have any idea where they might be?"

"WOULD WE BE STANDING HERE IF WE DID?"

We sat in the kitchen, where Dodi made tea for everybody. Grandma poured brandy into hers from the hip flask she always carries in her bag. She offered some to Officer Roberts but he said no thank you very much, he was working, and then he asked when the Babes went missing, and were there any relatives they might have gone to?

"YES, ME," Grandma hollered. "BUT I AM HERE."

"We think they may have gone to find Dad," I said.

"Where does he live?" asked Officer Roberts.

"He lives here, but most of the time he is in Warwick," I said.

"Where is your mother?" asked Officer Roberts.

"She also lives here but most of the time she is abroad," said Flora.

"So who looks after you?" asked Officer Roberts.

"Zoran," said Flora. "He's actually gone to Paris."

Officer Roberts asked us for photographs of the Babes, and he said they would put out a missing person alert for both of them. He said they would pay particular attention to coach and train routes to Warwick, and that the transport police would be on red alert, but that we had to understand that two feet of snow fell last night in some parts of the country and that it was absolute chaos out there. He also said he would have to alert Social Services. He said this was standard procedure, but he looked very disapproving when he said it. He said we should keep trying to get in touch with our parents and to let him know as soon as we had made contact.

"WHAT AND THAT'S IT?" asked Grandma.

"We will do all we possibly can," said Officer Roberts,

and then he left. Dodi hugged me and then she and Jake left, too.

That was at ten thirty this morning. Since then we have learned that most but not all of the trains to Warwick were canceled this morning, that some left London but never arrived, and that some were diverted onto other lines, so if Twig and Jas did try to catch one of them, they could be anywhere. Their photograph has been e-mailed to stations up and down both lines, but nobody has reported seeing two unaccompanied minors along either route.

It is late now, and dark outside. We have spent the whole day waiting. We kept trying to call Dad, but only got his answer phone. The snow, which seemed so magical this morning, has become unbearable, and the silence is deafening. There are no cars because of the snow, and no planes either. Mum has called several times, each time sounding more hysterical than the last. She is stuck at the airport in New York, crying and wailing in the departure lounge because her plane can't land at Heathrow. We have had to face the possibility that she might not be here in time for Christmas at all. We are all doing a grand job of pretending the Babes will be, but secretly I know we are all terrified that they won't. We don't say anything but we are all thinking about three years ago, when Iris went out alone in the dark.

Dad finally called and spoke to Grandma. We heard her

from all the way upstairs, "WHERE THE HELL HAVE YOU BEEN ALL DAY? YOU ARE UTTERLY SELFISH! I CANNOT BELIEVE YOU ARE NOT AT HOME!"

"It's not Dad's fault," said Flora. We stood together at the window in the Babes' room. It stopped snowing late this afternoon and now the sky is completely clear.

"No," I agreed. "It isn't."

"It's nobody's fault, is it?" said Flora. "Iris died and it was an accident and none of us have ever gotten over it. So in the end, we just fell apart."

"This isn't the end," I said. I breathed on the window-pane and it steamed up. Without thinking, I drew a heart with an arrow through it.

"Joss was at a party with Kiera last night," said Flora. "CJ posted photos on Facebook."

"I'm sorry," I said.

"No, I'm sorry. You were friends, and then I stole him. I didn't mean to—it just felt like such a long time since I'd been happy, you know?"

"It doesn't matter," I said.

"You must hate me."

"I don't hate you," I said. I looked at her, my crazy big sister, sitting in her striped pajamas and old cardigan with her weirdo hair piled up on her head, and I almost smiled. "I really, really don't," I repeated, and she almost smiled back.

Grandma went to bed at eight o'clock, though she said she couldn't possibly sleep. I tiptoed in a few minutes ago, and she was sitting upright in bed with her book on her lap and her hip flask on her bedside table, snoring. Flora is in her room talking to Tamsin on the landline. She has switched off her cell because she doesn't want to speak to Joss. I have been talking to Iris, wherever she is, asking her to look after Jas and Twig, who wherever *they* are right now will surely need all the help they can get.

There are only three of us in the house, when there should be at least nine.

My video camera lies on the bed where I left it this morning, ready to film the snow. My fingers are itching for it. It feels wrong, somehow, to film at a moment like this, and yet now the thought has entered my head I can't get it out.

It's too quiet. I am going out, and I am taking my camera with me.

THE FILM DIARIES OF BLUEBELL GADSBY
SCENE NINETEEN (TRANSCRIPT)
THE GRAND FINALE

PART 1

NIGHT. THE GARDEN GLEAMS, SNOW REFLECT-
ING THE LIGHT OF THE CRESCENT MOON. LADEN
BRANCHES HANG LOW. THIS DOES NOT LOOK LIKE
LONDON. THIS IS ANOTHER WORLD, A PLACE OF
MAGIC, OR IT WOULD BE BUT FOR THE SOUND OF
THE CITY COMING BACK TO LIFE AND A HELICOP-
TER CIRCLING OVERHEAD.

Snow falls to the ground as CAMERAMAN (BLUE)
brushes against boughs on her way from the house to
the rat runs at the bottom of the garden. Cameraman
crouches to film them. The BABES must have come
here before they left, because the cages are full of
fresh, dry straw and there are some barely touched
apples in the feeding bowls. Cameraman taps the top of
the females' cage. The straw packed into the sleeping
den rustles. A pink nose appears, twitches, and dives
again for cover.

CAMERAMAN
(whispers)
Petal, Betsy, do you know where they are?
Because if you do, you have to tell me. If you do,
you have to say.

JOSS
(off camera)
You know talking to rats is the first sign of
madness?

JOSS comes into focus as Cameraman straightens. He
wears a padded donkey jacket, his trademark beanie
pulled right down over his ears. The tip of his nose
is pink like the rats', his eyes sparkle. He grins and
waves, then hiccups.

JOSS
(hiccuping again)
I have braved snowplows and frozen trains to
wish Flora a Merry Christmas.

CAMERAMAN
(bravely)
I don't think that's a good idea.

JOSS
(staggers a few steps toward the camera then
stops, swaying)
But I love her.

CAMERAMAN
She's upset! Not just with you—oh Joss, the Babes
are missing! We think they've run away!

Joss stops walking. He bites his lower lip, deep in
thought. A few seconds pass.

CAMERAMAN
(almost sobbing)
We don't know where they are.

JOSS
(trying hard to focus)
I *have* to speak to Flora.

He holds up a hand to stop Blue's protests.

JOSS (cont.)
We have to pull our ressources. Pool together. Put
our differences behind us.

JOSS (clapping hands)

Come along, young Bluebell! Best foot forward!

Joss strides forward, slips on the ice, stands up again, and disappears into the house. Cameraman follows (feeling uncertain).

THE FILM DIARIES OF BLUEBELL GADSBY
SCENE NINETEEN (TRANSCRIPT)
THE GRAND FINALE

PART 2

INTERIOR, NIGHTTIME. THE LANDING OUTSIDE
THE CHILDREN'S ROOMS.

JOSS throws open FLORA's door. Flora screams and
drops the phone

> JOSS
> (grandly)
> I have come to help you find the missing Babes!

> FLORA
> (looking daggers, pulling duvet up to her
> shoulders)
> I said I never want to see you again!

> JOSS
> (falls onto bed, where he sits staring mournfully
> at Flora)

You're cross. I understand. I can explain. I love
you.

Flora struggles out from beneath the covers and stands
precariously on the bed. Joss tries to take her hand.
She pushes him away, leaps off the bed, trips and hits
her head against the edge of a shelf.

FLORA
(blood pouring down her face from cut on her
forehead)
Go away! Leave me alone! I hate you!

JOSS
(seizing Flora by the shoulders and shaking her
quite hard)
For God's sake woman, listen to me!

Flora yells and knees him in the groin. Joss doubles
over in pain.

CAMERAMAN
(her screams faint against the sound of the
helicopter outside)
Stop it! Stop it! Stop it!

GRANDMA appears in a scarlet dressing gown and mad hair, shouting IT'S A MIRACLE! IT'S A CHRIST-MAS MIRACLE!!! She points to the window. She cries, THERE IS A HELICOPTER IN THE SQUARE!! Camera pans right and through the dark and glass and trees does indeed pick out a small helicopter, which has now landed on the lawn of Chatsworth Square. Four figures stand beside it. Two men and two children. FATHER, TWIG, JAS, and A MYSTERIOUS OTHER.

> GRANDMA
> (finally noticing the three people in the room)
> WHAT IS GOING ON HERE?

> CAMERAMAN
> Daddy! Daddy, oh, Daddy!

Picture blurs as Cameraman runs downstairs. Cameraman's voice off-picture cries *Daddy, come quickly!* Father hovers briefly into view, looking faintly green after ride in the helicopter.

> FATHER
> What is it? What has happened?

CAMERAMAN

(beginning to cry)

Joss and Flora! Upstairs! She's bleeding! He's hurt!

For a moment, everything freezes. All eyes are on Father, who has just conquered his greatest fear, brought home two lost children in the middle of the night, and was not expecting this as a welcome home.

CAMERAMAN

DADDY!!

The scene unfreezes. Father roars and thunders up the stairs with Cameraman in hot, jolting pursuit, to Flora's room where Joss kneels on the floor, crying. Flora sits on the edge of her bed, her face covered in blood. His arms are wrapped around her waist, his head buried in her lap. She is also crying and tries to push him away. Grandma is whacking him on the head with a paperback, but he ignores her.

JOSS

I'm sorry, I'm sorry, I'm sorry!

FATHER

Let go of my daughter, you creep!

Father's fist connects with Joss's nose. Blood spurts everywhere. Father laughs, sounding mad. Commotion as Jas, Twig, and Mysterious Other enter the room, followed by OFFICER ROBERTS who, together with Mysterious Other, leap on Father to stop him from punching Joss again.

SATURDAY, DECEMBER 24 (VERY EARLY MORNING)

Just for a moment, in the garden with Joss, I thought he was going to surprise me. When I told him about the Babes, for a few seconds I thought he was going to come up with some crazy way of finding them. Stupid, I know, when you think of what happened afterward, but I haven't forgotten the incident with the rats. Joss just has that effect on people. Well, he had that effect on me.

After everyone had embraced everyone else, we crowded back in to the kitchen where Grandma made tea and cut enormous slabs of Christmas cake for everybody, even Joss who had to keep his head tilted back because of his nosebleed, and Officer Roberts who kept trying to tell Dad that he was under arrest, and in between hugs and mouthfuls of cake the Babes told us what had happened.

They did make it to Warwick—well, obviously, because they found Dad. Twig did some secret research online after he left my bedroom on Thursday night, and they left the house at four thirty, planning to catch the five-thirty train from Paddington.

"It was freezing," said Twig. "But it wasn't snowing yet. We got to Paddington no problem."

"We got the tickets out of the machine on the platform," said Jas. "And then we found a lady and sort of stuck near her so people thought we were with her. It all went fine until we got to Reading."

"But we didn't realize we had to change trains," said Twig.

"And then it started to snow . . ."

"And the train just stopped. For *hours* . . ."

"And we only had Christmas cookies and some ham sandwiches and an apple and two bananas and a Mars bar to eat . . . And then the train started again but it was the wrong one anyway . . ."

"So then we had to go back to Reading, which took *forever* . . .

"And then we had to change trains *again* and this time we got it right, but it was going so slowly it was like hardly moving at all . . ."

"And when we got to Warwick it was dark and we didn't have any money for a taxi and we didn't even know where Dad lived . . ."

"And then I started to cry . . ."

"It was very difficult," said Twig, "because we don't have cell phones. I do think after this we should. It's very unfair that we don't. We had to ask a complete stranger to call Dad for us. It's very lucky we know his number by heart."

"He felt sorry for me because I was crying," said Jas. "And then Daddy came to fetch us in the helicopter."

And then it was all eyes on Dad, who coughed and looked embarrassed, and the stranger who had arrived with them and whom Dad had just introduced as Herbie stood up and gave a little bow and said that, as it happened, the helicopter belonged to him.

"YES BUT WHO *ARE* YOU?" boomed Grandma.

"My name is Herbert Goldman," said Herbie. "I am a director of the Goldman Picture Company, and I am pleased to say that this afternoon we finalized a contract with your son to write a major motion picture set in twelfth-century Britain called *Daughters of King Arthur*."

"We were in a meeting with our lawyers all day, and my phone was off," said Dad. "I couldn't tell anyone before now because they swore me to secrecy, and also I didn't want to get anyone's hopes up. I've been working on it all term."

"Oh my God, the glasses!" said Flora. "The long hair! The phone! The designer jeans! All those crazy questions! We thought you were having an affair!"

"No!" Dad looked around the room at each of us in turn. We all nodded.

"I TOLD YOU YOU SHOULD SAY SOMETHING," said Grandma.

"Does Mum know?" asked Flora, and we were all quiet for a moment, thinking about Mum.

Mr. Goldman's phone rang at that moment, and he hurried out of the room.

"I'm sorry," whispered Dad. "I know it's been difficult, but you have to understand how much money they are paying me for this. To be honest, it's rather obscene. I've never seen so many zeros on a check. I've actually resigned from the University."

Mr. Goldman came back into the room and announced that his helicopter was going to take him to his hotel and did anyone need a lift anywhere? Officer Roberts looked sour and said that no, he and Dad were going to walk to the station, and Dad said he could stick his walk to the station. Officer Roberts said Dad should be careful not to add another resisting arrest to his long list of charges, which to date already includes both resisting arrest and assaulting a minor, which is when Grandma asked Officer Roberts WHAT ON EARTH HE WAS DOING HERE ANYWAY and it was his turn to look embarrassed as he said he came to tell us the children had been sighted at Warwick Station before being whisked away in a helicopter.

"We believed they had been kidnapped," he said with

dignity. "It's not the sort of news you want to give someone over the phone."

"Why didn't *you* phone when you found them?" Flora asked Dad.

"I tried," he said. "But the line was engaged."

"You are a danger to society and to these children," said Officer Roberts.

"You've got the wrong man," shouted Dad, which can be a good line in a film but in our kitchen sounded a bit overdramatic.

"I can prove it," I said. Everybody turned to stare at me then. I blushed and held out my camera. "He was only defending Flora. He was a hero. You'll see, I filmed every-thing."

SATURDAY, DECEMBER 24 (EVENING)

After he saw my film, Officer Roberts didn't take Dad to the police station but marched him and Joss around to his grandparents instead. He said he could understand how Dad got so angry, but that Joss was a minor, and even though it did look like everyone had been attacking everyone else, breaking his nose was a bit of an overreaction and Joss's family might want to press charges.

Mr. Goldman watched them go, looking thoughtful.

"Maybe one day we could make a film about your family," he told me, and he gave me his business card. "Call me if you're interested," he said.

And then he said good-bye to everybody and he was gone, just like that, in his helicopter.

Dad looked quite pleased with himself when he came back. He said Mr. and Mrs. Bateman weren't going to press charges and had finally admitted that Joss came to London because he kept getting into trouble at his old school, not just for pranks like the rats or bunking off class but for more serious things like stealing and drinking and getting into fights. Apparently he and CJ and Sharky and Spudz used to fight all the time, and the final straw for Joss's parents was when Joss punched someone in the face at a party because he didn't like the way the guy was looking at Kiera. His grandparents said how pleased they were when Joss started going out with Flora, because she seemed to have such a calming influence on him, but then when Dad asked why he and Flora were fighting Joss admitted that he had been lying to her about Kiera. She had finished with him after he hit the boy who was supposedly looking at her, but then she heard he was seeing someone in London and decided she still really liked him after all. So he started going out with her again, but then when Flora found out and yelled at him over the phone it made him really upset because he realized he really liked her, too. So, he came to

London to try to get back with her, as well, only things didn't quite go according to plan.

"Nobody messes my daughter around," said Dad. Flora started to cry again and said did we think she should forgive Joss or should she actually never speak to him again, and Grandma said IF YOU FORGIVE THAT BOY *I* WILL NEVER SPEAK TO *YOU* AGAIN.

It was a strange day. We all went to bed at about three o'clock in the morning, and when we got up it was properly Christmas. Grandma was cooking an enormous breakfast and Dad was making mulled wine. There was a fire in the grate and lights on the tree and there were the four of us, building a snowman in the garden.

But this is us, the Gadsbys. Christmas is different for us, and the snowman actually looked more like a snowgirl, because without consulting us Jas had gone into my old bedroom and taken Iris's red Father Christmas hat out of the box full of her things at the back of the wardrobe, the girl's one with the long blond braids hanging down the sides. We couldn't help laughing when we saw it, except then we all cried a bit as well because Iris used to wear it every single Christmas since she was about five years old.

"Was it wrong?" asked Jas. "Just, I look in that box quite often, and I thought it would be nice."

"Oh, Jazzy." Flora drew Jas into her arms for a kiss. "Of course it wasn't wrong. It's lovely."

"I look in her box, too," said Twig. "And sometimes I lie on her bed."

"I pretend my shadow is actually her," I said. "Sometimes I talk to it."

They all stared. "That's a bit mad, Blue," said Flora, but her smile got all twisted, and then Jas started to cry so loudly it was quite hard to understand what she was saying, but when I did I wanted to cry again, too.

"I don't remember her!" cried Jas. "I smell her clothes and I touch her things, but when I close my eyes I CAN'T REMEMBER WHAT SHE WAS REALLY LIKE!"

"Me neither," whispered Twig. "That's why I do it, too."

Flora wrapped her arms around both of them.

"Say something," she hissed at me. "Say something to make them remember."

I can't, I wanted to say. *I can't talk about Iris, I just can't.* But they all carried on looking at me, with their big round eyes and wobbly lips and pleading expressions, and suddenly I knew exactly what to say, and I started to smile.

"She was bossy," I said. "And she was fearless, and she was good at climbing trees. She never paid attention to anything anyone said, and she used to make us shampoo cats."

"Not just cats." Flora was smiling, too. "Dogs as well. Even, once, a gerbil."

"We had ice-cream competitions," remembered Twig. "To see who could eat the fastest. It used to give me a headache because of the cold, so she made me wear a hat."

"She taught me to ride on the living-room sofa," whispered Jas. "She made me sit on the arm and pretend to do the rising trot."

"She swiped all my best T-shirts," said Flora. "She sold them at the school fair, to raise money for Chinese pandas."

We sat out there together for ages, the four of us, snuggled up together in the snow, and every memory and story led to more memories and stories. The cold and wet seeped through our jeans and coats. Jas's lips turned blue and Twig's teeth started to chatter, but when the light faded and Grandma called us in, we didn't want to go.

She's still out there now, our snowgirl Iris, watching over the garden.

Watching over us.

There was a message from Mum on the answering machine this morning. She left it at ten thirty New York time, so just after we had gone to bed, saying that she had found a flight to Paris and that she wasn't sure how she was going to get to us from there but that she loved us very much.

"Paris?" said Flora.

We played it again. She did say Paris. Dad has been trying to call her all day. We know she is in Europe, because of the different ringtone, but we have no idea where.

"There are no trains," moaned Dad. "There are no ferries; the airports are still closed. What earthly use is it her being in Paris?"

"Maybe she's with Zoran," whispered Jas.

"Paris is a big place, pumpkin," said Dad.

She called at lunchtime and spoke to Dad.

"What did she say?" asked Flora.

"I couldn't tell," he admitted. "She was crying too much."

Twig answered when she called at teatime.

"Something about a tunnel," he said. "And a line, and a backlog, and having to wait."

Dad tried calling Mum back.

"Also," said Twig, "something about using someone else's phone because her battery is dead."

The doorbell rang at nine thirty. The Babes leaped off the sofa to answer.

"IT BREAKS MY HEART." Grandma actually wiped away a tear. "IT CAN'T POSSIBLY BE HER."

The rest of us crowded around the window to look. Flora shrieked.

"IT'S ZORAN!" she cried, and tore out of the room. By the time Dad and I reached the hall, the front door was wide open and snow was pouring in. Zoran stood on the doorstep in a shearling coat and his fur hat, with a Babe on each leg and Flora hanging around his neck.

"But, how?" said Dad. "I mean, why? And where . . ."

Zoran laughed. It's amazing how three weeks in Paris

can change a man. He's shaved off his beard for a start, and I have never seen him look so happy, not even at the piano.

He put a finger to his lips. "Shh," he said. "Come outside."

There was a new car parked in front of the house. By which I mean an old car, but one we had never seen before.

A Renault 5, said Twig, who notices such things, a model discontinued in 1991, with the steering wheel on the wrong side.

A Renault 5 with the steering wheel on the wrong side, and Mum asleep in the passenger seat.

"Shhh," said Zoran again. He was grinning from ear to ear. "She's been asleep pretty much since we left Dover."

So we got our Christmas, one way or another. Grandma made sandwiches and cut more cake, Dad heated more wine, and we sat around the fire until gone midnight. The Babes told the story again of how they went to fetch Dad in Warwick to bring him home. Dad told us all about Mr. Goldman, the film, and his new career as a screenwriter.

"I told you I could do it," he said to Mum, and she said she never doubted it for a moment, she just didn't understand why he couldn't do it at home. And then before they could start arguing Grandma said TELL US WHAT HAPPENED TO YOU, CASSIE. So Mum blew her nose and told us how she used up the last of her phone's battery to call Zoran, who came to meet her at the airport in a borrowed car, and just kept on driving north until they got to England.

"We waited for hours at the tunnel," she said. "I *told* you, when I phoned."

"I'm afraid I didn't really understand," said Twig.

"I'll drive the car back after Christmas," said Zoran. "When the snow has gone."

"But your family!" cried Flora. "Christmas!"

"It's all about the people you love," he smiled.

Grandma told the story of how Dad rescued Flora. Dad blushed and said, "I know I went a bit over the top," and Mum actually laughed. Zoran glowered and said he never did trust that boy.

"I'm never going away again," vowed Mum. "I don't care about Bütylicious and their stupid job. I'm never leaving *any* of you again," and Dad looked like he didn't completely believe her but was really happy just to hear her say that.

Me, I didn't say anything, as usual. I just watched. At midnight, Dad poured out more glasses of mulled wine, mugs of hot chocolate and cups of tea, and we drank to Iris.

"And to all others who've gone before us," said Grandma softly after we had drunk, and I knew she was thinking about Grandpa.

"To all others who've gone before us," murmured Zoran, and I knew that he was thinking about his parents.

He caught me looking at him, and I smiled. Then, because a smile did not feel quite enough, I slid out of my armchair and hugged him.

If this had been a film, it would have zoomed in on each of us in turn. When we drank to Iris, I saw how much it meant to all of us. Not just Mum and Dad and me, but to Flora and Jas and Twig and Grandma, too. So the camera wouldn't linger on any one of us. It would pan slowly from each person to the next and then it would pan outward until we were all in the picture, her parents and her grandmother and her twin and her other siblings, and a man who never knew her but who loves us, too, now, and who would have loved her if he had known her.

Iris's family. My family. All of us together.

SUNDAY, DECEMBER 25

A lot of good things happened today.

Today Mum and Dad kissed under the mistletoe. We had to make them, but once they started they didn't stop.

Today, somehow, despite late flights and snow and secret eleventh-hour film contracts, there were presents under the tree.

Today, Zoran and Grandma together cooked the biggest meal I think I have ever eaten, and after lunch we sang carols around the piano.

Jake came around while we were singing. He said he was dropping in on the way to the park because he was bored, like we didn't all know that for him to come this way is a massive detour. Nobody said anything, but Flora winked. He stayed for tea, and it was nice.

THE FILM DIARIES OF BLUEBELL GADSBY
SCENE TWENTY (TRANSCRIPT)
THE BIRTH OF BABY JESUS

VERY EARLY IN THE MORNING. THE HOUSE AND GARDEN.

Camera jerks up and down, revealing pajama bottoms tucked into four sets of snow boots, running as quietly as it is possible for snow boots to run down stairs, over the black-and-white marble of the hall, slowing to a more careful pace on the icy steps of the veranda and picking up speed again on the trampled snow of the lawn. Camera pans upward, still jerking every which way. FLORA runs ahead, her pink and green dressing gown hanging down beneath a thick gray fleece. TWIG and JAS follow, wrapped in blankets. Dawn is not far off and colors are still muted, the sky a soft pale blue streaked with pink and gold.

Camera stops, once more, by the rats' two cages. Very carefully, Twig opens the lid of the female rats' cage and separates the nest of straw in the sleeping hatch to reveal a nest of tiny baby rats, curled around each other.

TWIG
(triumphant)
I knew something was up! I sensed it! I knew they would come at Christmas.

JAS
Oh, *sweet!* Can we call one of them Jesus?

FLORA
But I thought this was the girls' cage! Joss said . . .

CAMERAMAN
Joss wouldn't know a female rat from a hibernating sloth.

Flora and BLUE begin to laugh. They laugh until the camera is shaking, tears pour down Flora's face, and she has to cross her legs so as not to pee. They laugh until the picture is filled with nothing but the snowy ground and the Babes laugh, too.

Their laughter gives way to gasps.

FLORA

Come on, let's go and have breakfast before
Zoran and Grandma get up and kick us out of the
kitchen.

Twig closes the lid of the rats' cage and follows Jas
and Flora into the house. Cameraman lingers a little
longer. When she is alone, she steps away from the
cover of the trees and raises the camera up toward
the balcony of next door's attic bedroom. A shadow
is up there, watching. Picture comes back down,
showing a view of the house from the back of the
garden.

CAMERAMAN

Wait for me, I'm starving!

Picture jerks as Blue begins to run. She stops at the
top of the veranda steps. Flora leans in to the picture
and plucks the camera from her hands.

CAMERAMAN (FLORA)

I've always wanted to have a go at this.

Picture goes in and out of focus. Blue's voice, off camera, tells Flora to give it back. Flora says no. Picture

continues to dance, then settles on close up of Blue's face.

    CAMERAMAN (FLORA)
    Gotcha!

Camera zooms closer still until the screen is full of nothing but Blue's laughter.

Camera goes black.

    THE END

TURN THE PAGE FOR A PEEK
AT NATASHA FARRANT'S NEXT NOVEL

THE FILM DIARIES OF BLUEBELL GADSBY
SCENE ONE (TRANSCRIPT)
SUNDAY DINNNER

INTERIOR. EVENING.

The Gadsby family kitchen in the basement of the
big house in Chatsworth Square is a mess. Bubbling
pans crowd the stove. A collapsed chocolate cake
balances on top of a fruit bowl. The sink is piled high
with dirty dishes. Water drips, steady and unnoticed,
onto the floor. FATHER sets the table, looking grumpy.
FLORA sits at one end of the sofa under the window.
She wears leopard-print leggings, an emerald-green
sweater, and the fedora she has refused to take off
since she had her hair cropped and dyed peroxide
blond last week on her seventeenth birthday. She is
reading a play. At the other end of the sofa, nine-
year-old JASMINE is her complete opposite—tiny, with
tangled black hair falling down to her waist, a long
black tunic over black jeans, and silver high-tops. She
is reading a poem called *The Raven* by Edgar Allan Poe.

1

MOTHER, covered in flour and melted chocolate, stands by the cooking range. She is flustered. She tastes the content of a pan (tonight she is making goulash), burns her tongue, and throws the spoon in the sink.

NOTE 1: For the past year, Sunday night dinner has been prepared by ZORAN, the Gadsby family's au pair, who started out being able to cook nothing but sausages, but by the time he moved out a month ago he became a seriously good cook. He is coming for dinner tonight for the first time since he left to become a full-time music teacher, and Mother is determined to make an impression.

FATHER
I should be writing my book. I should not be setting tables. Remind me again why we are doing this?

FLORA
(smirks, still reading her play)
Mum wants to show us she cooks just as well as Zoran.

MOTHER
I am simply throwing together a meal for an old friend.

2

FATHER

It doesn't look simple to me, it looks . . .

MOTHER

What?

FATHER

Excessive.

Mother glares at Father. For a moment, it looks like
she is going to throw the goulash at his head, but then
a football sails in through the garden door (left open
despite the cold night air because it is so hot in the
kitchen), followed by TWIG.

The football crashes into the set table and breaks several glasses.

*NOTE 2: Since Twig turned eleven last summer, the family
joke is that his legs have grown so fast he doesn't know
what to do with them. And sure enough, no sooner does
Twig burst into the room after the ball than he trips over
his legs, and ends up sprawled on the floor, leaving a trail
of mud and wet leaves.*

TWIG

(somewhat awestruck by the damage he has done)

I swear I didn't do that on purpose.

Telephone rings. Mother answers, looking increasingly dejected as she murmurs phrases like "of course I understand" and "please let us know if there is anything we can do to help."

MOTHER

(hangs up the phone, looking like she wants to cry)

That was Zoran. Someone has had a heart attack. He's not coming.

FATHER

(surveying the ruined table)

After all that?

MOTHER

David, someone has had a *heart attack*.

She notices CAMERAMAN for the first time.

MOTHER

Blue, what are you doing with that camera?

CAMERAMAN (BLUEBELL)

I'm starting up my diary again.

MOTHER

Turn it off, *now.*

I have noticed that people only write in diaries when there's something wrong, write properly I mean. Over the past few months I've only used up about half a notebook, and most of those entries are all "I can't believe how long it's been since I last wrote" or "oh dear I feel guilty because the holidays are over and I haven't once opened this note-book," but today I have got right back into it because Mum and Dad are fighting again. Last year, when Zoran came to live with us as our au pair, we were falling apart because my twin sister, Iris, had died three years before and we still missed her so much, but things started to get better after he arrived. In fact, they improved so much that when he tried to resign last Christmas, we wouldn't let him go. Even after Mum and Dad decided to leave their old jobs so they could be at home more (Dad is a full-time writer and Mum works for a smaller makeup company that doesn't make her travel), he stayed with us right up until the summer, when he finally completed his PhD in Medieval History and told us it was time for him to move on.

"I cannot be a nanny forever," he explained when we asked him why. He has been giving music lessons all year, and now he wants to be a full-time music teacher.

At first, after Mum and Dad resigned, they made a real effort, not just with us but with each other. They stopped fighting and started to slope off for romantic weekends in the country instead. Apparently they had a lot of catching up to do, and it just wasn't possible to be romantic with four children in the house. Flora said it was a scandal. She said that at seventeen she was the one who was supposed to be skulking off to canoodle in secret, and that they were making a complete spectacle of themselves, but they were happy, so we didn't mind. And then, around about when Zoran left, Mum and Dad's canoodling stopped. This morning they had a huge fight, and they have barely spoken to each other all day. Flora says we should Resign Ourselves to the Inevitable. We were all quite ready for the parents to divorce last Christmas, and apparently the intervening months have been no more than a Temporary Reprieve.

I don't know if Zoran leaving and Mum and Dad quarreling are related. I just know that even though he wasn't always very good at looking after us, things were better at home when he was still around.

The reason Zoran didn't come for dinner is that the grandfather of one of his students has had a stroke. The difference between a heart attack and a stroke, Dad says, is that a heart attack is what happens when blood stops flowing to the heart, and a stroke is what happens when blood stops flowing to the brain.

"So it's a brain attack," Twig said, and Dad said yes, he supposed it was.

"But why does that mean Zoran couldn't come for dinner?" Jas frowned.

"Because he was at the boy's house giving a music lesson when it happened. The boy lives with his grandfather and has no other family. Zoran offered to look after him." Mum stared at the goulash, the green beans, the potato gratin, the red cabbage with apples and raisins, the chocolate cake, and the custard and sighed.

"Those poor people," she said.

"Is the grandfather going to die?" Jas is fascinated by death. "Will the boy be an orphan?"

"I'm sure it won't come to that," Mum said. "Please stop asking questions."

"I still don't get why they couldn't come for dinner," Twig said.

Flora said, "Oh, what, Zoran should have been like, I know your only relative just nearly died but why don't you come and have dinner with a group of total strangers?"

"We're not strangers," Twig said.

"I can't imagine only having one relative," I said. "That's so sad."

As usual, nobody listened to me except for Mum, who gave me a little smile. Zoran says every family has a child who is less loud than the others, and sometimes I feel like I'm invisible. Maybe it's because unlike Flora and Jas, I don't have statement hair and clothes. My hair is brown and normal, my clothes never seem to go together, and at fourteen I'm still wearing the little round glasses I got when I was twelve, but I don't really care about any of that. I just wish once in a while someone would pay attention when I finally get a word in edgewise.

"But why is Zoran looking after him?" Jas ploughed on. "I thought he didn't want to be a nanny anymore. If he was still living with us, would that mean the boy with the grandfather would come and live here too? Couldn't they come and live here anyway?"

"STOP ASKING QUESTIONS!" said Dad.

"She's only asking because she's wants to know," said Mum.

"You just told her exactly the same thing."

"That was different."

"No it wasn't."

"Yes it was."

"Sometimes," Jas said, "I wish *I* were an orphan."

"That is a terrible thing to say," Flora scolded, but then she added that sometimes she did too, and everybody sulked for the rest of the evening.

MONDAY, NOVEMBER 4 (THE FIRST DAY OF HALF TERM)

Jake has asked me to go out with him. He left for Australia

9

today, to go to his auntie's wedding. The holidays are only a week long, but because Australia is so far away and it is A Genuine Family Reason as well as a Highly Educational Trip, God (aka Mr. Kelly the headmaster) has given Special Dispensation for him to stay away for a month. On Friday Tom, who along with Colin is still Jake's best friend for reasons I sometimes find hard to understand, was all, "WHAHAY, DUDE, NO SCHOOL FOR A MONTH AND THINK OF ALL THOSE HOT SURF CHICKS," but Jake went all serious and then this morning he said could I meet him at the Home Sweet Home café before he went to the airport, and he asked me.

Clearly, I am not invisible to Jake.

"The thought of a whole month without you," he said, "made me realize how much I like you." He asked if I would wait for him and I nearly choked over my cappuccino because, even though I've known Jake since primary school, I have never thought about him in that way, and it was the last thing I expected him to say. He taught me to skateboard last year when I was still so unhappy about Iris, and he's been one of my best friends ever since, but being best friends with someone is not the same as going out with them. I was trying to find a way of telling him that but then he said, "Blue, are you okay?" and he looked so worried and nervous that instead I said yes, going out with him would be very nice.

As soon I got home I climbed onto the flat roof outside my bedroom window to call Dodi (it's the only place in our house where you can be really private). Dodi is about as different from me as a best friend can get. She's blond and girly, she loves fashion, and even though she's never actually had a boyfriend, she's very interested in boys.

"Tell me exactly what happened," Dodi said.

"He said, would I wait for him, and then he kissed me on the cheek and held my hand for a bit and made me promise to e-mail him every day."

Dodi sighed and said that made us practically married.

"It wasn't very passionate," I said.

Dodi says that's because we are such good friends. She says it's hard to be passionate when you know someone so well, but after a month apart, the flames of our passion will be *incandescent*.

Seriously. Incandescent. Dodi is the sort of person who has an opinion on everything. I can't imagine how it would feel to be like her, always so sure that you are right.

"So you think I should go out with him?" I asked.

"You've already said yes, haven't you?" She sounded really excited. I tried to explain about friends not being the same as boyfriends and everything, but as well as always having opinions, Dodi also often doesn't listen to me.

"You two are going to make the cutest couple," she said, but then our conversation was interrupted by my family starting to scream at each other in the garden.

"What's going on *now*?" Dodi's parents are very quiet, and she doesn't have any brothers or sisters. She is endlessly fascinated by us.

I crept to the edge of the roof. Beneath me, Dad stood by Twig and Jas's pet rats' cage, surrounded by the rest of my family, who were all yelling.

"I'll call you back," I told Dodi.

What happened was, Dad let the rats escape this morning. Normally Jas feeds them, but she was staying with her friend Lola last night, so Dad said he would do it, but then he forgot to close the cage and they ran away. Jas found the cage wide open when she came home.

Dad tried to defend himself saying the rats were probably happier living free as God intended. Jas cried, "But they are not used to the wild." Dad said Chatsworth Square was not exactly the wild, and Jas started to sob that her heart was broken forever, which is when Mum jumped in saying, "Really, David, murdering the children's pets is the last straw."

"I did not *murder* them!" cried Dad. "It was an accident! And they are rats! They can live anywhere!"

All seven of the rats have escaped. Twig, who had promised to sell Betsy's babies to his friends, informed Dad he had ruined his career. Jas cried even harder because she hadn't even realized Betsy was pregnant, but nobody was listening to her because Dad was yelling "Freedom! Freedom!" like some deranged rat revolutionary. Mum said he couldn't use political idealism as an excuse, especially applied to rats, and then he started waving his arms around crying how no one understands how difficult it is for him to be locked in his study all day trying to write a novel and knowing that the responsibility for his ENTIRE FAMILY'S WELL-BEING rested on his shoulders, and we all tiptoed away because it was clear our father had finally lost his mind.

I e-mailed Jake before writing this, to tell him all about it. Now that I have agreed to go out with him, I feel that I should tell him everything, even though it's not always easy to find the words. Nobody wants people to think their father is a lunatic. Then I called Zoran to see if he could help, but he says there is nothing he can do. Rats, once they are gone, are gone forever, in Zoran's opinion.

His student's grandfather from last night, who is called Mr. Rudowski, hasn't woken up from his stroke yet. His student, who is called Zach, is still staying with him because even though Zoran has tried to call the boy's mother, she hasn't replied.

"Zach says she lives abroad," he said.

"How come he lives with his grandfather?" I asked. Zoran said it was complicated.

"Why hasn't she replied?"

"I don't know, Blue. Believe me, I wish she would."

I wish Zoran would come home and live with us, but unlike Jas, I have no desire to be an orphan. I'd rather have two parents yelling at each other than no parents at all.